"I don't require a salary," Megan said softly

Every last dime he had probably went toward Susan's medical bills. "Room and board will be enough."

Bitter pain flashed in Richard's eyes. "This house suffers from abuse and neglect. Do you honestly think a scrubbing brush can erase it?"

"No." Megan's calmness became an accusation. "Your house has to become a home to do that."

His whole body reacted as if she had struck him. Then he straightened his shoulders and turned away. "All right, stay if you want," he said curtly. "I'll give you the room and board you asked for—but I won't believe you don't want any money. Your kind of woman always has a price!"

Books by Maura McGiveny

HARLEQUIN ROMANCE
2511 – DUQUESA BY DEFAULT
2679 – MEGAN'S FOLLY

HARLEQUIN PRESENTS
674 – A GRAND ILLUSION
723 – PROMISES TO KEEP

These books may be available at your local bookseller.

Don't miss any of our special offers. Write to us at the following address for information on our newest releases.

Harlequin Reader Service
P.O. Box 52040, Phoenix, AZ 85072-2040
Canadian address: P.O. Box 2800, Postal Station A,
5170 Yonge St., Willowdale, Ont. M2N 6J3

Megan's Folly

Maura McGiveny

Harlequin Books

TORONTO • NEW YORK • LONDON
AMSTERDAM • PARIS • SYDNEY • HAMBURG
STOCKHOLM • ATHENS • TOKYO • MILAN

Original hardcover edition published in 1984
by Mills & Boon Limited

ISBN 0-373-02679-X

Harlequin Romance first edition March 1985

CHAPTER ONE

MEGAN closed the door of the art gallery behind her and stubbornly lifted her chin, refusing to let her disappointment show as she joined the pedestrian traffic on Hindley Street. That was the last gallery on her list and they couldn't help her. So where did she go from here?

For the past six months she had heard the same thing from everyone remotely connected with art, from galleries to art supply stores to private collectors. Methodically going down her list, she tried them all, and not one of them had seen her portraits or could tell her of anyone else who might have done.

'Sorry, Miss Crane,' was the familiar response. 'If you'd care to leave a description of them along with your address and phone number, we'll get in touch with you if we hear anything.'

It was difficult to accept defeat. It had been a wild goose chase from the start, she would have admitted it months ago if she hadn't been so stubborn. That was her biggest fault. All the nuns knew it. Mother Superior had told her the odds were against her, but Megan had had to come ten thousand miles to try to prove her wrong.

When the prestigious New York art gallery informed her that the portraits had been sold inadvertently to someone from Adelaide, she was staggered. Those paintings had been on loan; they weren't supposed to be sold. But a new employee had made a mistake. The man came in to the

5

gallery during the noon hour and had paid cash. No one else saw him, and the only thing the salesgirl could remember was that he was handsome and he spoke with a gorgeous Australian accent and had remarked that he was returning home to Adelaide that day.

It was a futile exercise, but Megan had to come, hoping to find him and buy the paintings back. That was six months ago. Now what? She didn't want to give up and go home yet. Her chin came up. That wasn't her style. Maybe someone would answer the ad she'd put in today's paper. If she had to, she'd get a job and stay here and continue searching. Everything would work out all right. It had to.

The sunshine was blinding as she turned with new determination and briskly crossed the street. Her hair slipped out of its dark red knot and when she pushed it out of her eyes a wave of dizziness suddenly swept over her. It took her a minute to shake it off and she smiled ruefully. She would have to have more respect for this climate. The month of January in Adelaide was a lot different from January in New York—so much warmer than she expected. A thin trickle of sweat ran between her breasts and she daringly undid several buttons at the front of her white cotton dress, hoping a breeze would find its way in to cool her heated skin. The heat didn't seem to bother any of the other people filling the sidewalk as she scanned the sea of suntanned faces all around her.

Not looking where she was going, she collided with a warm solid object and for a dazed second she stood swaying.

'Excuse me,' a deep voice murmured from somewhere far above her head. 'Are you all right?'

He was a man, a tall one, and broad, she realised, lifting her eyes from the buttons of his wrinkled blue shirt past the tanned skin of his neck to his face. There she was caught by a pair of the bluest eyes she had ever seen.

'I'm sorry,' she said, strangely breathless, not wanting to drag her eyes away from his.

Both his hands impersonally fastened on her upper arms, gently moving her out of the way. As he noticed her dress gaping open and glimpsing her lush figure beneath, his mouth thinned slightly before he lifted his wide-brimmed felt hat and nodded to her. Settling it back on his head, he drawled: 'You really should watch where you're going. A little thing like you could get hurt.'

The timbre of his voice was deep and soothing and ran over Megan's jangling nerves like the soft slither of satin. She wondered who he was and what he did as she watched his tall figure turn and melt into the crowd. Knowing there was no chance of ever finding out, she gave herself a mental shake and again started forward before stumbling over something at her feet. A man's wallet lay there. Reaching down, she turned the crisp brown leather over and over, then quickly scanned the crowd. He must have dropped it when she collided with him. If she hurried, she just might catch him before he got swallowed up in traffic.

'Oh, mister!' she called, running blindly in the direction he had gone. 'Wait!'

But it was a full two blocks before she caught up to him and she was out of breath and panting when he turned, frowning, to face her. 'I think you dropped this,' she said, a self-satisfied smile lighting up her face. His legs were twice as long as hers, but she'd managed to catch him.

Not returning her smile, he reached into the hip pocket of his jeans and brought out a worn black wallet. 'Nope. Not mine.'

'Oh.' She was crestfallen. 'I thought you dropped it back there . . .' Her voice trailed off uncertainly at the grimness gathering in his face.

'Look, miss, I'm sure this is a novel approach, but I'm not interested.'

Megan looked at him, blinking in bewildered confusion. A sound of disgust rumbled deep in his throat before he turned on his heel and left her without another word.

'Nice try,' a tall woman standing in an open doorway drawled softly with admiration. 'But you can't win them all.'

Megan turned to her and felt a sudden embarrassed heat rush to her face. She hadn't realised anyone had witnessed the rebuff. 'Er—I really did think he dropped his wallet.' She lifted her shoulders helplessly.

The woman smiled in sympathy and came closer, taking the obviously new wallet and inspecting it. Her hair was piled in a bright mass on the top of her head and it reminded Megan of the colour of carrots. A slinky purple dress, slit up one side, clung to her curving figure. She was young, maybe in her mid-twenties, and although a thick layer of make-up hid most of her expression, her brightly painted mouth was stretched in a friendly grin. 'It's empty—no money, no identification. But then there wouldn't be, would there?'

Megan looked nonplussed.

'I wasn't born yesterday, you know. The men you're trying to pick up aren't going to fall for it either.' She tilted her head to one side. 'You're new here, aren't you?'

Megan nodded warily, not understanding her at all.

The woman laughed softly. 'I'll give you a word of advice, then. That innocent air of yours won't fool them for long, so drop it. You don't have to pretend you found their wallet to strike up a conversation. Just be yourself and let them see a little of what you've got. They'll take one look at you and beg for more.'

Megan's eyes widened as all at once she realised what this woman was and what she thought Megan was. Her heart fluttered to her throat and stuck there. She'd heard the term 'ladies of the night', but she'd never had the occasion to actually meet one before. Fascinated rather than repelled, she kept looking at her.

'What's the matter? Is my lipstick smudged or something?' The woman reached into a sequin-studded bag and pulled out a mirror, primping her hair with long scarlet fingertips.

'Er—no.' Embarassed that she'd been caught staring, Megan couldn't very well say she had never come face to face with anyone like her before and was shocked yet at the same time curious. It might hurt her feelings. The woman wore a lot of make-up, but she seemed so nice and friendly, not at all hard, the way her type was portrayed in films and on TV. 'Er—thanks for the—advice.'

'Oh, that's all right,' the woman laughed. 'Always willing to help a friend. You look a nice kid but still inexperienced. Give it time.'

Hectic colour flooded Megan's face. What could possibly make her think such a thing? She looked nothing like this other woman. Always conscious of her shortcomings, she was more aware of it now next to this woman. She was too short, for one thing, and she didn't know how to wear make-up. Her eyes were a brilliant green and her skin a pale colourless white that wouldn't tan even in this hot sun. Her hair was long and wild and dark red and her figure on the round side, with hips too wide and breasts too big for her diminutive height. Altogether, she didn't add up to anything spectacular like this tall curving flamboyant woman in front of her.

The she suddenly held her breath as she watched her turn away to smile at a handsome cowboy walking towards them. He eyed both girls with quickening interest before smiling at Megan. Her heart galloped to her throat and she turned away at once, swiftly re-buttoning her dress all the way up to her chin, and almost ran to the bus stop, hotly embarrassed but not being able to do a thing about it.

The bus ride home didn't take long and her face was still a bright red when she climbed the stairs to her flat. As she inserted her key in the door, she heard the phone ring and unquenchable hope surged through her. It has to be an answer to my ad already, she thought, quickly putting her first brush with the seamier side of life out of her mind.

The man on the other end of the phone had a pleasant voice, husky and deep, and she liked the sound of it. What she didn't like was some of the things he was suggesting. Her face fell and her eyes widened and her heart began to race in confusion.

'What did you say?' she asked incredulously, thinking she had misunderstood him.

When he repeated the obscenities, a hot surge of embarrassment swept over her before she gasped and put the receiver down without a word. Dazed, she stood breathing heavily before opening the newspaper she'd bought on her way home. Turning to the want ads, she scanned the section and found it. It was just the way she had worded it. There was no mistake.

But more than two hours later she realised what a mistake it was. Now when the phone rang she was afraid to answer it. Hot angry tears stung her eyes and she clenched a fist against her mouth to keep from sobbing. How could she have been so stupid? Why had no one told her about these things? This was a side of life she never knew existed. One of the nuns had once told her they had done her a disservice by keeping her so sheltered. At the time she hadn't realised what she meant, but now it was all becoming so clear.

She swallowed back her panic and tried to get a grip on herself. If only she had somewhere else to go, someone to turn to. But she was alone, on her own in a vast country where everything was unfamiliar, even the seasons of the year. A gnawing emptiness shivered through her as she realised just how vulnerable she was.

'Megan? Are you in there?' a feminine voice called through the door.

A gentle tapping combined with the ringing of her telephone and she stood for a long minute not daring to answer either.

'Megan, it's me, Lora. Are you all right?'

The phone stopped and she finally took a deep breath and opened the door to the girl who lived in the neighbouring flat.

Lora was a long-standing acquaintance and the complete opposite of Megan. Tall and slender, she laughed a lot and was unselfconscious and full of starry-eyed expectancy. She looked at Megan's swollen eyes and blinked in astonishment. 'I was just on my way out and I couldn't help but hear. Is something wrong?' She was hesitant, unwilling to pry yet wanting to help.

Not trusting herself to say anything, Megan shuddered and handed her the newspaper before nervously wrapping her arms around herself and crossing the small room to stand by the window with its view of one of Adelaide's many parks in the dusky twilight.

Lora frowned. The paper was opened and folded to the want ad section. 'I don't understand. I know you told me you were going to place an ad for your paintings, but what's in here to make you cry?'

Just then the phone started to ring again and Megan jumped guiltily. 'Don't answer it!'

'Why?' Lora looked at her stricken face and frowned. 'Do you know who it is? Is it some kind of bad news you don't want to hear?'

Megan shook her head and fresh tears slid down her face.

'For heaven's sake, what is it?' Lora was becoming more and more puzzled, and finally, after ten rings, she couldn't stand it any more. She picked up the telephone, looking at Megan, and firmly answered it: 'Yes? May I help you?'

There was only silence and Megan watched all the colour drain from Lora's shocked face as she stood absolutely still, listening. Then a sudden dull red washed up her neck before she slammed the receiver down with a loud crash.

Megan hiccuped back a sob. 'I told you not to answer it.'

'Have you called the phone company? They have ways to stop obscene calls, you know.'

'This was my own fault.' She hunched her shoulders dejectedly and scrubbed at her eyes. 'But I honestly didn't realise——' Her chin came up. 'Read the ad I put in the paper. It's in the second column, halfway down.'

Lora's forehead wrinkled as she looked at the paper in her hand. Then her face changed when she found it and she gasped. 'Megan! You can't be that naïve!'

'I never thought,' she cried shakenly. 'Oh, I could just die!'

'I know you're desperate to find them, but to actually *say* so in the paper! And to say you're willing to do anything to get them back! Good lord, you must have realised all the weirdos would come crawling out of the woodwork?'

'No, I didn't know. I had no idea. But I should have. Oh, what am I going to do?' Megan almost wailed.

Lora let out her breath and stared at her, then her face changed, became almost pitying. 'All right, all right, it's not the end of the world. Take the phone off the hook for starters. When they ring back they'll find it's engaged and after a while they'll give it up. If they don't, you can always change your number.'

'Oh, Lora, its not that easy. What if this person finds out who I am and where I live and comes here?'

'Of course he won't. People like that just get their kicks over the phone. You've never had an obscene call before, have you?'

She shook her head and shuddered violently.

'Poor Megan! One can be frightening enough, but I take it you've had several?'

'Every fifteen minutes since four o'clock this afternoon.'

Lora's swiftly indrawn breath was harsh and eloquent. Putting her arm around Megan's shoulders, she suddenly felt very old and motherly, even though she was only nineteen and Megan had to be at least two or three years older. 'I'm meeting Jerry for dinner in half an hour. How about coming along? Now's not the time to be alone.'

Megan bit her lip. 'I couldn't impose on you like that.'

'It's no imposition. This isn't a special occasion or anything. I meet Jerry like this every Thursday night. Besides, what are friends for? Jerry's seen you a couple of times in the hall and he always asks how that "knockout of a readhead" is. He'd love to meet you, I know it.'

The phone started to ring again and Lora grimaced at Megan's sudden convulsive shudder. 'Go wash your face and put on something comfortable. The restaurant isn't fancy. That'll come later, once Jerry's established a flourishing medical practice.'

Megan gave her a watery smile. 'How can I thank you——'

'Go on.' Lora briskly pushed Megan to her bedroom, waving away her gratitude. 'And leave your hair loose,' she called. 'Jerry'll like it that way. When the phone stops ringing, I'll take it off the hook.'

While she was waiting, Lora let her gaze wander around the tiny flat. Exceptionally clean and functional, there was nothing here to make it uniquely Megan's. She wondered about that. The furniture was faded but comfortable, mismatched cast-offs provided by their landlady, Mrs Simpson. The sofa was chintz-covered with a lumpy cushion in the centre. An overstuffed chair was in a corner,

and if it was anything like the one in her own flat
next door, she knew it would have matching lumps
too. There were no pictures on the stark white
walls and nothing but an empty glass vase on an
end table. Nothing in the room spoke of the shy
quiet girl who lived here.

Lora had taken an instant liking to Megan when
she moved in six months ago, but she had never
really known much about her except that she was
an artist from New York City and she was
searching for two paintings she had done of a little
boy that had been sold by mistake. She never
dated anyone and kept to herself most of the time,
yet she was friendly and didn't act as if she had
anything to hide. Some of the things she said and
did made Lora think she was as innocent as a
newborn baby, and this latest stunt proved it
beyond a doubt. Lora could laugh it off, but
Megan was deep. She had a feeling it would take
her a long time to get over it—if she ever did.

Five minutes later Megan came to stand in front
of her with a hesitant smile. 'Is this all right?'

'Wow!' Lora skimmed over her lush curves. 'It's
a good thing Jerry loves me and we're engaged to
be married! If we were just dating, I'd worry that
he'd drop me like a hot potato once he meets you.'

'You would?' Megan looked down at the simple
green jersey dress and frowned, wondering what
Lora saw that she had missed. 'It's not too dressy?'
she asked at last.

Lora smoothed her hands down the sides of her
nearly straight figure in a beige peasant style dress
and smiled. 'You're the type who could wear a
burlap bag and make it look gorgeous. No, it's not
too dressy. It's your figure that gives it class. Even
when you wear your old paint-stained jeans, you

manage to turn men's heads. Come on—I can't wait to see Jerry's face!'

The compliment should have made Megan feel flattered, but she could only wonder why other people saw her so differently from the way she saw herself.

They were nearly at the bottom of the stairs when a door off the entrance hall opened and their landlady peered out.

'Megan, I want a word with you.'

'Can't it wait, Mrs Simpson?' Lora spoke up quickly, taking one look at her icy eyes and sensing calamity. 'We're meeting Jerry and we don't want to be late.' She tried to shepherd Megan past her, but the woman stepped in front of them, blocking their way.

'You may go, Lora. I want to speak to Megan.'

'But we're going together . . .'

'What I have to say won't take long.' The landlady's imperious tone bounced off the walls and her tall angular figure seemed to fill the tiny hallway as she glared at Megan. 'This is a respectable house, Miss Crane. I've lived here all my life and never before have I run into this situation.'

It was then that Megan saw the newspaper in her bony hands. 'I can explain——'

'This doesn't require an explanation,' she cut her off, her thin lips tightening with displeasure. 'I have a long waiting list of respectable girls who wish to rent my flats. I sympathise with your desperation, but I won't tolerate such goings on. You have until five o'clock tomorrow to find another place to live.'

Megan's face fell. 'But, Mrs Simpson——'

'I'm not about to stand here and argue with a

common trollop!' The woman tossed her iron grey head haughtily and stepped back into her own apartment, leaving the two girls staring after her.

'Self-righteous old bitty!' Lora muttered under her breath. 'Come on, Megan.'

When she would have hung back, Lora gripped her arm and hustled her out of the door and down the broken sidewalk. 'Don't take it so hard. In a few days you'll probably look back and see that she's done you a favour. Her rent's exorbitant anyway. I'm only staying here because I'll have to move when Jerry and I get married and no sense doing it twice.' She tried to be reassuring, keeping up a lighthearted chatter, but it was difficult to ignore Megan's stricken look. 'It's going to be a gorgeous night. Let's walk instead of taking a chance on my old Volkswagen, okay? It's not far and the exercise will do us good—well, me anyway. You don't need it, that's for sure.'

Megan followed her down the quiet tree-lined street in the deepening dusk like a silent ghost. This can't be happening, she thought. Twice today she'd been mistaken for a loose woman. And both times she hadn't been able to defend herself. If it hadn't been so ill-timed, it might have been funny but now not only was she fast losing all hope of finding her paintings, she didn't have a home any more either. What could she do? Where could she go? All of a sudden a long-forgotten clutch of abandonment swept through her. She was alone; there was no one to really care what happened to her. All her life she had been alone, but she thought she had mastered the sense of loss and despair long ago. Why did it have to come back now when she least expected it? The nuns are my family, she told herself. They care. I'm not alone.

A fine sweat appeared on her forehead and her
breath became shallow.

'Megan?' Lora's light touch on her arm brought
her back to her surroundings and she forced
herself to breathe deeply and not give in to panic.
That wouldn't help anything.

They had stopped in front of a half-timbered
building with latticed windows meant to look like
an old English pub.

'Cheer up, Megan. Jerry might know of
someone who's looking for a roommate—one of
the nurses or aides or something. I really believe
everything happens for a reason. Just be patient
till you find out what it is.' Lora smiled
reassuringly, pulling open the door and stepping
inside, motioning for her to follow.

It was all Megan could do to force an answering
smile to her face. Instinct had her looking for a
place to hide to lick her wounds in private—but
she'd have to wait until later for that luxury. Lora
would think she was ungrateful.

The restaurant was softly lit and cosy, catering
to families as well as couples wanting intimate
tables, and it seemed as though every available
space was taken. People were spilling out of the
wide wooden booths along the walls and were
jammed at the tables clustered around an unlit
hooded fireplace in the centre of the big room.

As Lora glanced around looking for Jerry, a
waving hand caught her eye. 'Come on, Megan.'
She gently took her arm and urged her forward.
'Look at the way Jerry's eyes are dancing! He can
hardly wait to meet you.'

They weaved their way through a maze of
tables, and Lora automatically slid into the booth
next to Jerry before she realised he was not alone.

Two men were seated opposite him, and one of them got up at once to let Megan have his seat.

'I'll get a chair and sit on the end,' he said with a goodnatured grin, ushering her into his place with a practised flourish.

Megan shyly thanked him and looked at Jerry, then glanced at the other man in the booth next to her and stiffened abruptly, her eyes widening in shock. He was the same man she had seen earlier in the day with the wallet. Those blue eyes of his were unforgettable. He still wore the wrinkled blue shirt and she saw his raven-dark hair, which had been hidden by his hat earlier, was smooth against his head. His nose was straight and there were deep slashing grooves at the sides of his mouth and he had a deep cleft in his chin.

He hadn't forgotten her either, by the looks of him. All at once his lip curled and his cold eyes ran over her body with insulting thoroughness. The blatant sneer he threw at her set her heart thumping wildly against her ribs.

Lora, not noticing, made the introductions. 'Megan, I'd like you to meet my fiancé, Jerry Nolan, and his best friend, Richard Talbot. Jerry, Richard, this is Megan Crane.'

Megan was motionless, her mind tripping all over itself wanting to explain to Richard Talbot that she wasn't at all what he thought. But she knew if she said anything it would probably involve long explanations and only make matters worse, so she sat as far away from him as she could and held her tongue. Dragging her eyes away from those icy blue ones, she forced her mouth to curve in a small smile and looked across the table to Jerry. 'It's a pleasure to meet you. Lora's talked about you often.'

Jerry Nolan, a brash young man with curly dark hair and dancing eyes, quickly flashed her a brilliant smile. 'I knew today was my lucky day. Now I can celebrate in style, with two gorgeous women and my best friend and the man who made it all possible. Jim's just offered me the chance of a lifetime.'

Lora's eyes rounded as she looked from Jerry to the man coming back with a chair.

He was older, in his middle forties, while Jerry and Richard couldn't be more than thirty. He had dark brown hair that was thick and curling near the collar of his white shirt. Like Jerry, he had a dark tie knotted loosely around his neck and the top button of his shirt was undone. He was not a handsome man, but he was attractive in a comforting way. Tiny lines crinkled at the sides of his eyes when he smiled, and Megan knew instinctively here was a man people could trust.

'Megan, this is Doctor Jim Crawford, chief of staff at the hospital where Jerry works. Jim, Megan Crane.'

Warm brown eyes rested on her. 'My pleasure, Miss Crane.'

Lora couldn't contain her curiosity and quickly dragged his attention back to her. 'What did Jerry mean?' she asked. 'The chance of a lifetime?'

His lips quirked as he looked from Megan back to Lora. 'I needed a good right hand, and Jerry's the best up-and-coming surgeon I know.'

'You're going to work with Jim?' She whirled around to face Jerry, radiant with happiness. 'And we can stay here in Adelaide instead of going to Perth like you thought? And we can be married now instead of having to wait until next year?'

His head bobbed up and down. 'Right on all

accounts, darling. This is where we'll be living. I take it you don't mind?'

'Mind? Are you kidding?' In her happiness she beamed at all of them, then threw her arms around Jerry, kissing him soundly without being the least bit embarrassed.

'Congratulations,' Megan said softly, happy for them.

Jim Crawford grinned, then glanced sideways at Megan, struck by her bittersweet smile and Richard's cold withdrawn manner.

'Oh, Megan,' Lora shook her head and sighed when she came back down to earth, 'it isn't right that I should be so happy when you're so miserable.'

Jim's eyebrows rose in a question, but he didn't say anything.

Just then a waitress came to take their order.

'This was supposed to be a beer and pizza night,' laughed Jerry. 'But that's a little mundane for a celebration, isn't it?'

'Not at all,' answered Jim, knowing the salary of his friend bordered on poverty and also knowing Jerry would insist on paying for the meal. 'Beer and pizza for everybody?' He glanced around the table.

Not wanting to draw any attention to herself, Megan nodded in agreement. She had never tasted beer before, but there was a first time for everything.

Richard quirked a dark eyebrow after the waitress left. 'Somehow you don't look the beer and pizza type, Miss Crane,' he couldn't resist taunting, his long fingers tracing the rim of his empty beer mug. 'Wouldn't you be more at home with champagne cocktails and Chateaubriand?'

She looked up quickly and her eyes clashed with his for a long disturbing moment. 'The name's Megan,' she said uncomfortably, 'and you don't really know my type at all.'

Lora heard them and had to laugh. 'You could never tell by looking at her that she's an artist, could you, Richard? And Megan's as down-to-earth as they come.'

Insolent blue eyes ran over her face and probed her body with a provoking expression as he tilted his head to one side. 'I find it hard to picture you starving in a garret, Megan.'

A miserable red ran up her neck as she was reminded of her roundness compared to his lean frame beside her. Even in his jeans and wrinkled shirt she could tell there wasn't an ounce of fat on him. For the second time that day, she wished she was tall and slender like that woman in the purple dress she had met earlier.

Sensing a strange undercurrent of constraint between them, Jim came to her rescue. 'Where are you from, Megan? That's definitely not an Australian accent.'

'I'm from New York City,' she said in a quiet voice.

He smiled. 'What brings you all the way out here? Just visiting? Or are you making it permanent?'

'I'm not really sure. I'm going to have to get a job so I can stay in Adelaide and keep looking for some paintings of mine. I can't leave until I find them.'

'*You're* the girl Lora was telling us about?' Richard broke in coldly, his voice faintly incredulous.

She felt him stiffen beside her before she flashed a questioning look to Lora.

'I hope you don't mind,' Lora said quickly. 'I thought I'd be helping if I asked around for you. I might run across them in a place you'd miss.'

'I hadn't thought of that,' she sighed.

'They're portraits, aren't they?' Richard asked, his lip curling. 'Of a boy about three years old?'

She nodded, and for some reason felt she had just fallen several more notches in his estimation.

'Why don't you put an ad in the paper?' Jerry added, trying to be helpful, but all that got him was one of Lora's sharp elbows in his ribs.

Megan wanted to sink through the floor. 'No, that wouldn't do at all. I'm through putting ads in the paper.'

Jim moved to one side to allow the waitress to put the pizza on the table and Megan was spared having to make humiliating explanations while she helped to pass the plates and mugs around.

'Eat up, Megan,' Lora flashed a smile to reassure her. 'You don't want to end up with bigger problems than you've already got!'

'This isn't a night for problems.' Jerry leaned forward with a flourish, deftly lifting slices of pizza from the elevated tray in the centre of the table, sliding them on to the plates. 'There's magic in the air. Can't you feel it? Tell us what the trouble is and one of us will make it right again.'

'Our landlady told her she has until tomorrow to find somewhere else to live,' Lora said quickly, not really taking him seriously but knowing Megan's reticence would make her keep silent.

A low whistle came from Jerry's throat as he held out a brimming plate. When Richard reached for it, his arm brushed Megan's and it was hard to tell which of them flinched more at the unexpected contact.

Only Jim noticed and his eyes narrowed thoughtfully. 'You do have a problem, don't you? There's no solution on the horizon?'

'Not that I can see,' she admitted, lifting her chin. Her hands wrapped around her beer mug almost defensively. Not about to admit defeat in front of all these strangers, she smiled brightly. 'But I'm sure something will turn up.'

'Maybe I can help you—with a job and a place to live if not with finding your paintings,' said Jim. 'What kind of work are you looking for?'

'Anything——' she started to say, before a dull red blush crept up her neck. She looked at Lora. 'That is, anything within reason.'

'It just so happens I'm looking for a nurse——'

'—No, Jim!' Richard stiffened incredulously and cut him off with a flat denial. 'I know what you're thinking and it won't work. Look at her—she wouldn't last a week.' His eyes ran over her again, narrowing on the lush curve of her breasts before grimly returning to Jim. 'Besides, a girl like her wouldn't have to look for a job very long. She's used to a different kind of bedroom care.'

Lora gasped, but the insult went right over Megan's head.

'Oh, please,' she said quickly, 'if you need nursing help, I'd be glad to do it. I've got to find a place to live and if I could help you at the same time . . .' She looked from him to Jim and back again, wondering why they looked so strangely angry with each other all of a sudden. Something was going on beneath the surface. Swirling undercurrents of hostility were running riot all around her.

'Why not give her a chance?' Jim Crawford said quietly. 'It would solve both her problem and yours. She'd have a job and a place to live, and you'd have a nurse for Susan.'

Lora looked at Megan and shrugged with a deliberately expressionless face. If she knew what was going on, she wasn't going to say anything. Jerry simply sat quietly beside her, watching everything.

A peculiar tension gripped them, and finally Megan moved. Ignoring Richard's angry stillness, she put a timid hand on Jim's arm. 'I'm not a trained nurse, but I have cared for sick people before,' she said softly. 'Terminally ill patients.'

'Ah.' He smiled straight into her eyes. His hand covered hers and it was warm and firm and she felt strangely comforted. 'Come to my office at the hospital tomorrow morning at nine o'clock for an interview. I'll give you all the particulars then.' He flicked a look at Richard as if daring him to say something, but Richard merely turned away in disgust before his eyes collided with hers, boring right through her with something she couldn't fathom.

Open bewilderment flashed in her face, but when she opened her mouth Jim cut her off at once. 'It'll keep until tomorrow,' he said kindly, lifting his beer mug to toast Jerry. 'Right now, let's help Lora and Jerry celebrate.'

CHAPTER TWO

MEGAN slept badly that night, which wasn't surprising. Richard Talbot's grim face kept haunting her dreams. The job Jim Crawford had offered her had something to do with him and he made it obvious he didn't consider a woman like her suitable for it. If only she could have explained . . .

As she showered and dressed the next morning, the corners of her mouth tilted. She had to let her sense of humour surface; if she didn't, she'd start crying and never stop. If only Richard knew how wrong he was! She wasn't a woman with loose morals, but explanations were totally out of the question now. As last evening progressed, she had damned herself beyond all redemption in his eyes.

The beer she drank went straight to her head and without realising what was happening, she found herself relaxing indolently in the booth next to him with all her worries fading away. Normally quiet and extremely shy, she smiled expansively and even joined in a lighthearted banter with Lora and Jerry and Jim—all the while batting her eyes at Richard. Whatever possessed her to do such a thing, she'd never know. But it seemed the more grim looks he threw her way, the more determined she was to make him smile—and finally he did, and the effect was devastating.

Someone else had stopped at their table then, another doctor who was aware of Jerry's good fortune. He was promptly invited to join them, and as he began sliding into the booth next to her, she moved in to give him room and unthinkingly pushed up against Richard. Her shoulder pressed against his arm, trapping it between them until he lifted it to rest on the back of the seat. That only served to bring her closer to his wide chest, and when her thigh brushed the length of his, she became breathlessly still, acutely conscious of an indescribable thrill running over her body. Her instinctive response to his nearness was a mixture of naïve curiosity and a stangely confused yearning. The rest of the evening was hazy, but the remembered feel of that hard heated body burning the side of hers was as clear as if he was next to her right now.

Sober this morning, she shuddered, deeply ashamed, and pressed her hands to her hot face. This would never do. She had to forget about Richard Talbot and see about finding a place to live. Not with Jim Crawford—that was impossible now, but with someone else. She had to stay in Australia and find her paintings. That was what she had come here to do, and nothing would sidetrack her from that purpose.

Rehearsing a pretty little speech about why she couldn't accept his offer of a job, she made her way to Jim Crawford's office, smoothing her hands nervously down the sides of her navy blue skirt and blazer. She owed him that, at least. Her reasons had nothing to do with Richard Talbot, she would tell him, but rather, she wouldn't feel right in taking advantage of this new-found friendship. That ought to satisfy him and let her off the hook as well.

Jim's office was wide and spacious with dark walnut panelling complementing a soft honey-

coloured carpet on the floor. Two walls were made
up of floor-to-ceiling windows and he smiled,
spotting her through his open door. Standing with
the phone to his ear, he waved her to one of the
comfortable leather chairs in front of his littered
desk.

'. . . that's just not possible, George,' he said,
continuing with his phone conversation while
throwing her an apologetic look. 'I'm without my
secretary at the moment and things are beginning
to pile up on me. Ring me again in a day or two,
will you? I may have things sorted out by then.'

He rang off and seated himself behind his desk
with a frustrated sigh. 'It never fails. Whenever a
nurse walks out on Susan, my secretary has to fill
in, and then all hell breaks loose around here. I
can't run this hospital without her.' He dragged
his hands through his hair and his mouth twisted
morosely. 'And I suppose you only showed up this
morning to tell me you've decided not to help me
out after all?'

She sat up straighter, suddenly at a loss. 'How
did you know?'

'It's the way my luck's been running.' He sighed
again. 'Well, go ahead. Give me the speech you
must have spent half the night preparing,' he said
distractedly.

Megan's jaw fell open. She stared at him for a
full second and then started to smile. 'You don't
really want to hear it, do you?'

He smiled back, a warm smile dancing with
mischief. 'I'm sure it doesn't mention the real
reason, does it?' His eyes travelled over her in
gentle appraisal from her dark red hair caught in a
thick coil at the back of her head to her crisp navy
suit to her shapely legs in sheer stockings and

black high heels. 'You can't take this job because Richard Talbot thinks you're a hooker, right?'

She gasped and put a hand to her mouth, not quite expecting him to put it so baldly.

'Sorry, Megan. I know nothing could be farther from the truth—but tell me, how did Richard ever come up with that idea?'

She shifted uncomfortably in her chair and nervously twisted her hands in her lap. 'I found a wallet yesterday after literally bumping into him. I thought it was his and I'm afraid I chased him two blocks, trying to give it back.'

He frowned.

Her shoulders lifted and bewilderment was written all over her face. 'He said it was a novel approach but he wasn't interested.'

'Good lord! I know he's had his share of troubles with women, but I never thought it had left him that twisted!' Jim let out a long slow breath. 'And of course the cynic never gave you a chance to explain?'

She shook her head. 'By the time I realised what he meant, he was already gone. Besides, how could I even begin to explain something like that?'

He made a sympathetic noise. 'I see what you mean. So what are your plans, then? Have you done anything about finding a place to live?'

'No.'

'I wish I had the time to help you look.'

'Thanks anyway, Jim. You've been more than kind.'

'Kindness has nothing to do with it. I was looking out for my own interests. I need my secretary back but I also need someone to care for my patient.' He injected a slight note of pleading and watched her through hooded eyes.

Megan hesitated, wanting to help him but knowing it was impossible.

He saw her indecision and pounced. 'Change your mind, Megan. Richard's not a bad sort, really. He's had a tough time of it, what with his father dying unexpectedly and leaving his affairs in such a tangle and Susan's illness progressing faster than we thought. And then there's his little daughter, Charlotte——'

'He's *married*?' Stunned, she could only look at him. She knew Jim was married; his wife had been mentioned several times last night. And Jerry was engaged to Lora. But Richard! For some reason that had never occurred to her until now and her stomach plunged. But of course, she should have realised. The fact that he'd been alone didn't mean anything. A man his age and with his good looks must be married. And all the time she was batting her eyes at him, he must have been laughing at her. Her humiliation was complete now. Of all the boneheaded things she'd done since leaving New York, this had to be the worst.

'He's a w——' Jim was cut off by the ringing of the telephone and he grimaced, reaching for it with an exasperated sound.

Megan barely heard the one-sided conversation. Her thoughts were whirling. Some nun she was going to make, she thought with dismay. Last night she was practically in Richard Talbot's lap, rubbing up against him, actually enjoying—no, savouring—the feel of that warm muscular body against hers. She remembered wondering for one tantalising moment what it would be like to be held in his powerful arms and kissed by his hard mouth. That was when he had smiled at her again and she had smiled back, dizzy with pleasure. The memory of it pulsed through her even now, curling to every tingling nerve ending. And all the time he was married. He even had a daughter.

By the time Jim had finished his call, Megan's mortification was too great for her to do anything but sit rigidly in her chair and pray that this interview would soon be over.

'Now, where were we?' he said with a preoccupied frown, sifting through some papers in front of him. 'Oh yes, I almost had you talked into helping me. Please, Megan, take pity on a poor overworked doctor.'

'I can't, Jim.' She could never face Richard Talbot again.

'Why not?' He saw her chin wobble and shook his head. 'You don't have to worry about Richard, you know. You'll rarely see him. He doesn't spend much time in his house—he's got more than enough keeping him busy in his vineyards.'

'Vineyards?' Her head came up with a jerk.

'Why, yes. He lives in the Barossa Valley, outside Nuriootpa, about an hour's ride from here. It's one of our most famous wine-growing regions.'

Her eyes widened. 'He makes wine?'

'He grows grapes and sells them to the wineries.' His mouth drooped. 'Don't tell me you're one of those people who thinks Australia is nothing but long flat stretches of sunburnt land overrun with woolly sheep?'

Her breath came out in a rush. 'The classic "Ugly American", you mean?' Her mouth twisted. 'I don't know why I'm surprised to hear you have vineyards. Look at Adelaide. It's so different from what I expected—all the beautiful green parklands sprinkled all over the city and the way the River

Torrens runs through the centre——' She broke off and shook her head ruefully. 'Are all Americans who come to your country like me?'

'Not all. I haven't run across another one who's offered to help an overworked doctor.'

'Jim——'

'Please, Megan. I know I'm trying to wear you down and take advantage of your good nature, but admit it, I've got you intrigued. With the geography of the place, if nothing else.'

'You know just where to aim your arrows, don't you?' she said, trying not to sound chagrined.

He chuckled and settled back in his swivel chair, pursing his lips and making a pyramid of his fingers over his flat stomach. 'I'm simply desperate—and so are you. You need somewhere to live; I need help—it's as simple as that. And the Talbot place is near enough for you to be able to keep looking for your paintings. I'll even run you into town myself on days when I make house calls, and Susan isn't too bad. How about it?'

'But you need a nurse and I'm not one.' She was grasping at straws and they both knew it. 'You don't know anything about me.'

'So tell me.'

She frowned at him and suddenly felt very small and wished she hadn't come.

Jim frowned, sensing her reluctance, and sat up. 'All I know about you is that you're an artist from New York looking for some paintings sold by mistake. You've lived in the same building as Lora for the past six months and you're clean and quiet and keep to yourself. Apart from that——' he spread his hands, 'I don't think you're deliberately hiding anything. You're just a very private person, that's all. So tell me how you came to care for those terminally ill patients you mentioned last night. Or did you only say that for Richard's benefit?'

Megan stared at her hands clasped in her lap, then resolutely lifted her chin. 'No, it's true. It was in the infirmary in St Ann's Convent in New York City.'

He looked stunned. 'You're a *nun*?'

'Not yet. But I hope to be.'

He couldn't believe it. His jaw started to sag, but he snapped it shut and sat bolt upright. 'You hope to be,' he echoed incredulously, staring at her for a full minute. Then he threw his head back helplessly and started to laugh. 'And Richard thinks you're a hooker! Wait'll I tell him!'

'Please don't,' she whispered, mortified.

He grinned, savouring his enjoyment. 'Why not? I can't wait to see his face when he finds out how wrong he is.'

'Maybe he's not wrong!' she burst out, remembering the way she had behaved last night and wanting to die. Her face was full of bewildered pain and she put a clenched hand to her mouth. 'Maybe I won't make a good nun after all. Mother Superior told me she didn't think I had a vocation. I didn't want to believe her, but maybe she's right. Maybe there's a latent—hooker—in me.' She shuddered. 'After last night——' A sob choked her and she couldn't go on.

'Oh, Megan, it was only natural for you to turn to someone after all you went through yesterday——' A light tap on the door stopped him and he let out a harsh breath, looking up, clearly resenting the intrusion.

A woman was standing in the open doorway in her crisp nurse's uniform.

'Yes, Sharon?'

'Sorry to interrupt you, Doctor, but I'm on my break and I thought you might need someone to help answer your phone this morning?'

'Oh, thank you,' he said with relief, walking to the door. 'If you'd take their numbers and tell them I'll ring back later, I'd appreciate it.'

'Certainly,' she smiled.

Jim closed the door just as the phone rang and with a grimace he came back to Megan. Leaning against the edge of his desk, he looked down at her and tried to ease her distress. 'Tell me about it,' he said kindly.

She pulled herself together with difficulty, wanting someone to lean on yet knowing it was unfair to burden him with her troubles. He was a stranger, after all, and besides, he had enough of his own. 'This is not the confessional,' she said with a nervous little laugh. 'And you're really too busy to have to bother with me.'

He just smiled and put a reassuring hand on her shoulder and gently squeezed it. 'Sometimes it helps just knowing another person cares.'

She tried to smile back and swallowed. He was such a kind man; it was there in his eyes. Maybe he would understand. And maybe by telling him she would sort it all out in her own mind. 'Mother Superior told me I don't know anything about life,' she said softly, 'so it would be wrong for me to enter the order now. She wanted me to go out and see what the world was really like first. She said my paintings told a lot about me and she was sure I didn't have a vocation to be a nun.'

'But you think you do?'

She nodded. 'I thought so—until yesterday. And now I don't know any more. I'm so confused. One of the nuns told me it was probably just my stubborn streak that made me want to stay. Mother Superior refused my request, so I'm out to prove her wrong.'

He frowned at her. 'What made you think you'd want to be a nun in the first place?'

'It's the only life I know.'

His eyebrows shot up.

'I was abandoned on their doorstep when I was about four,' she said softly in a flat detached voice. 'The nuns should have sent me to a foster-home, but I kept telling them someone would come back for me. Mother Superior asked the Bishop for a special dispensation to let me stay for a few weeks and got it. After that, no one came to take me away from them, so she never said anything either. That was twenty years ago. The day before I left to come to Australia, she told me she'd done me a disservice by keeping me with them—I was too sheltered, there were so many things I wouldn't know.'

Jim ran a hand across his face trying to understand but feeling as if he was somehow becoming entangled in filmy cobwebs. 'But the boy in your paintings? If you've lived the life of a nun—in a convent—how did you—how could you have—a child?'

Megan blinked innocently wide eyes, surprised at his discomfiture before what he said made any sense to her. 'He isn't my son!' she gasped. 'How could you think that?'

His gaze fell from her face to the ripeness of her figure. 'Don't they have mirrors in convents?' He noisily cleared his throat and shook his head, more and more baffled. 'So who is this child, then?'

'He was just a little boy who came to the park every day to feed the pigeons. I started sketching him and we became friends.' Her face changed. 'Then one day he stopped coming and one of the ladies whose daughter played with him told me he'd been adopted. I never saw him again. Nobody could tell me anything—where he went or who'd taken him. The paintings were all I had left. And now they're gone.'

Jim Crawford let out his breath in a heavy sigh. 'I'm sorry, Megan. Lora told us about you and I'm afraid all of us jumped to the same conclusion—that you were an unmarried mother. It's a common enough thing these days, but that's no excuse. God, I can see now how you came to put that add in the paper!'

'You know about that too?' Her face burned with added humiliation.

'Jerry told me this morning when we made our rounds. Lora was so worried about you last night. She told him after they dropped you off. I must say, I didn't think anybody could be so innocent in this day and age. Now I understand.'

Megan leaned forward in her chair and looked straight into his face. 'But if I tried to explain all this to Richard, he wouldn't understand, would he?'

His mouth twisted. 'No, I don't think he would. He's too much of a cynic when it comes to women. He's already got you pigeon-holed, and once he makes up his mind, there's no changing it.' Getting to his feet, he crossed to the windows, looking out to the manicured lawn in front of the hospital before jamming his hands in his pockets. Then he took a deep breath and turned back to her. 'So, what are you going to do, then?'

She stood up. 'It's not your worry, Jim. I'll just have to think of this as part of the real world I'm supposed to experience. But thank you for listening to me. You were right, talking about it did help.' She knew nothing had changed, but she didn't feel so alone any more. Jim was busy and it was time to leave. The lights on his phone were flashing and she could hear the nurse becoming harassed on the other side of the door.

He warmly enveloped the hand she extended. 'Then this is goodbye?'

She nodded and tried to smile before turning to the door. It had to be goodbye. She couldn't stay and help him; she'd made such a fool of herself already, and staying would only make it worse. Richard Talbot thought she was a loose woman as well as an unmarried mother! She couldn't face him again. But when she left this office she knew she'd never see Jim or Lora or Jerry again either. She'd find a different place to live, different people, different surroundings. She'd lose contact with the only friends she had in Australia. As she fought back a sickening curl of desolation, her throat started to ache and she swallowed past the knot gathering there. This was nothing new. She should be used to it by now. All her life she'd never been able to get past the fringes—in the convent yet not really part of it. Certain rooms in the building were off limits to her and then there were all those different religious ceremonies, all the rituals she could observe but never take part in. She was the stranger, always on the outside looking in. Suddenly the thought was too much to bear. She didn't want to be alone any more. She wanted to belong somewhere, with someone, if only for a little while.

'Jim?' she swallowed nervously, her hand trembling on the doorknob.

'Yes?'

'Do you really think I wouldn't see much of Richard if I took your job?' She turned hesitantly, as if propelled against her will, and looked at him.

She didn't see the flare of relief in his eyes; she only heard the gentleness in his voice. 'I don't think you'd see much of him at all. He's never been the most sociable person in the world at the best of times. He prefers his vines to people. The only reason he was in town yesterday was that he brought back the last nurse I hired two days ago.'

'Two days?'

He nodded wearily and motioned for her to have a seat again, his forehead wrinkling in a frown. 'I can't understand it. None of the nurses I hire stay very long, and it's becoming more and more difficult to find someone. I've already used every available resource open to me. That's why it doesn't really matter that you're not a nurse—I'm that desperate. As long as you're willing to help and have a general idea of nursing care, that's all that's required.'

'Why don't they stay?' Megan asked haltingly, subsiding on the edge of the chair.

He looked at her for a few minutes as if weighing his words, then sat down heavily behind his desk. 'I've asked, but they never tell me—at least, not the real reason. All they'll say is "She's more difficult than I thought". But they were aware of that before they took the job. I just don't know what's going on out there, Megan. Maybe if you try, I'll get a straight answer out of you.'

A shiver of foreboding ran down her spine, but she fought off the sensation. 'Well then, if I'm going to try my luck, you'd better tell me what you do know.'

He smiled. 'All right. For openers, her name is Susan Shea.'

'Oh.' A warm look came into her eyes. 'Like the actress.'

'No, not like her. She *is* the actress.'

'*The* Susan Shea?'

'The one and only.'

'But I thought she died three years ago!'

'That's the statement she had me give to the press when the diagnosis of multiple sclerosis was confirmed,' Jim explained. 'She realized her acting days were numbered and rather than have people watch her deteriorate on screen, she went into seclusion.'

Megan was stunned. Susan Shea was world-famous, the idol of millions. 'I didn't know,' she said.

He nodded with gentle understanding. 'That's the way she wanted it. She's only thirty-two, the same as Richard, but she looks closer to sixty now. Her case is unusually severe and more rapid than most. She's completely bedridden. I give her six more months at most.'

He watched her absorb this in silence and when she didn't comment, he went on, 'It won't be an easy job taking care of her. She's always been a pampered woman and now she's next to impossible. Not only will you have her artistic temperament to contend with, but the Talbot place is somewhat isolated as well. Do you still want to help me?'

Megan lifted her chin and took a deep breath, burning her bridges behind her. 'I'm a lot tougher than I look, Jim. Is there anything else I should know before I start?'

'Just one more thing.'

'Yes?' She waited.

'Susan Shea gets absolutely livid if she's called Mrs Talbot. She prefers that stage name of hers even though she'll never act again. You might keep that in mind.'

There was no suitable reply to that, so she merely nodded, wondering what Richard Talbot thought of a wife who preferred a stage name to his own.

CHAPTER THREE

By four o'clock that afternoon, Megan was ready to leave for her new job. Jim Crawford had her redirect her mail to his office and simply disconnect her phone. If anyone wanted to contact her about her paintings they'd have to go through him first, he told her fiercely, and she smiled at this protective gesture and warmed even more to him.

Taking one last look around the small rooms she had called home, she closed the door quietly behind her.

'Make sure you take only what belongs to you, Megan!' Mrs Simpson shouted unnecessarily from the bottom of the stairway.

Jim Crawford juggled a box and a large suitcase down the narrow stairs and ignored the woman's stare of contempt.

'I'm sorry there had to be this misunderstanding between us, Mrs Simpson,' said Megan, handing her the key.

She tossed her head and sniffed. 'There's no misunderstanding. I knew you for what you were right at first—still waters and all that. I'm just surprised it took you so long to show your true colours. How could you settle for a man like that one?' Her face twisted into a sneer as she watched Jim stow Megan's few belongings in his sleek silver sports car. 'He's forty-five if he's a day and I'll bet that thick hair of his is a wig. I suppose he's wealthy, judging by that fancy car. Do you expect him to set you up in some fancy apartment and buy you all kinds of outlandish things without a thought for the poor unsuspecting wife he must have at home?'

Megan's face burned. 'It's not at all what you're thinking. I'm going to work for him.'

'Oh, it'll be work, all right. You'll find that out soon enough.' The landlady turned back to her own apartment, taking her indignation with her.

Megan winced as the door slammed in her face. I wonder what she'd say if I told her I intend to become a nun some day, she thought, her lips twitching in an irreverent smile.

'All set?' Jim held the car door open for her just as Lora drove up in her battered Volkswagen.

'Megan! I hoped I'd catch you before you left.' She bounded over to her, nearly tripping on the sidewalk, and grinned at her. 'Jerry called me at work and told me you were taking the job. You'll keep in touch, won't you? When Jerry and I are married, I'd like you to come to our wedding. Promise me you will.'

'I'll see to it she does,' Jim spoke up.

'Here, Megan, something to remember Jerry and me by.' Lora pressed a tiny box into her hands and then started back to her car. 'My boss only gave me an extra fifteen minutes, so I have to get right back to work.' She waved and with a noisy sputter, her car disappeared down the street.

Jim watched Megan gingerly open the box and had to smile when her face turned a becoming pink.

'Look, Jim.' She held up a necklace with a delicate gold rosebud on a slender chain. 'Isn't it gorgeous?'

He nodded warmly, wondering with a touch of

Richard's cynicism if there was any other woman in the world who would be pleased with such a simple, inexpensive gift.

Once the city of Adelaide was left behind, Megan realised she was unconsciously fighting a curious mixture of apprehension and anticipation. I can do it, she told herself, forcing herself to swallow back a sudden nervousness. She had decided on a course and she would stick to it, no matter what all the nurses before her had done. She'd think of this as a challenging adventure, a facing of reality, as Mother Superior had said.

They drove through the countryside and a comfortable silence fell between them. Megan watched Jim Crawford's hands on the steering wheel, not at all unnerved by him being on the right side of the car and driving on the left side of the road. The taxis back home in New York always had the driver's seat on the left side while driving on the right, and she wondered how long she had been taking such opposites for granted.

She had been expecting to pass through vast empty plains with desolate stretches of unbroken wasteland dotted with dried-up salt lakes, but Jim had told her that kind of landscape was much farther north. Here, there were gently sloping silver fields of wild oats and ripening hay on a road lined with squat date palms. The sun was high above them in a wide blue sky and heat shimmered gently all around them. In the distance, low grey-green hills were dotted with sheep and well-kept cottages with geraniums on their sills.

'It's all so beautiful,' she marvelled softly, 'so big and endless. I feel as if I can breathe again.' As soon as she said it, she caught her breath and turned suddenly guilty eyes on Jim. 'Now why do you suppose I said that?'

'Were those convent walls closing in on you?'

'I never felt that way before,' she said haltingly, 'and I'm not sure I feel that way now. Do you suppose Mother Superior knew something I didn't?'

He shrugged sympathetically but couldn't answer her.

After a while the landscape changed and she could see they were coming into a shallow valley with neatly laid out rows of low iridescent green vines heavy with ripening fruit.

'It's not much farther now,' he said, as if answering an unspoken question. Glancing at her sideways, he saw her hands clenched on her lap. 'Don't worry, Megan. You'll do fine.'

A nervous smile crossed her face. 'Somehow I don't think it's going to be that easy.'

'Having second thoughts?'

The powerful car began to slow and Megan knew all she had to do was say the word and he'd turn around and take her back. 'No. I told you I'd try. I'm not about to quit before I've even begun.'

'You're sure?'

Something in the way he said it made her heart start to thump unsteadily. She tilted her head sideways and tried to read his face. 'Is there something you're not telling me?' she asked.

'What makes you think that?'

He kept his eyes carefully glued to the road and she knew something was not quite right. A shiver ran down her spine. 'I don't know. You're acting—strange all of a sudden.'

He shot her a delving look, then just as quickly

looked away. 'I underestimated you. I didn't think
you'd be so perceptive.'

'Tell me!' Her eyes flashed and the heavy weight
of her hair slid out of its coil to surround her face
like a wild red halo. She was suddenly afraid and
she knew he could see it and it made her angry.

Jim whistled with surprised admiration and his
low throaty laugh scraped along her nerves. 'I
didn't think you had the temper that goes with the
red hair!'

'It's a fault I'm working on,' she said shortly,
letting out the breath she didn't realise she was
holding. 'Tell me what's wrong, Jim. I've been
honest with you. The least you could do is be the
same with me.'

'You're right.' His pretence vanished. 'It's
Richard. I rang and told him you were coming.'

'And?' she prodded.

'He's very much against it.'

'I already knew that.'

'Yes, well, I have a feeling he might try to make
things—difficult.'

'You mean more difficult than they already
are?'

'I don't know what I mean. I just have this
feeling——' He broke off and his hands tightened
around the steering wheel helplessly. 'I can't
understand it. He was so adamant. He doesn't
want you there, but I told him he had no choice in
the matter.'

'And what did he say to that?'

'What could he say?'

Megan bit her lip and kept looking at him as if
his face could tell her something. 'Is he that self-
righteous that the thought of a woman of my
moral calibre coming into his home——'

'Don't, Megan!' A loud sound of disgust cut her off.

'Don't forget, he thinks I'm a—a——' she floundered, trying to remember the word he had used this morning.

'Well, we both know you're not. When we get there you can tell him you intend to be a nun. That ought to set his mind at rest, if that's what's bothering him.'

All of a sudden her chin lifted mutinously and her mouth twisted. She wouldn't waste her time on useless explanations he didn't want to hear. 'No, Jim. If he thinks I'm like that, let him. It's his problem, not mine.' Her eyes flashed a brilliant green. 'Don't say anything to him. I'll let him know how wrong he is in my own good time.'

He shook his head, but didn't have time to say any more as he came to a crossroads and turned down a narrow dirt lane winding its way through flourishing, moist green vines lush with fruit, their leaves rustling in the breeze.

A few minutes later they pulled to a stop in front of a large, paint-blistered, two-storey house standing neglected in the hot sunshine. The front lawn was strewn with surprisingly high weeds and there were bare patches of sunbaked earth showing through the overgrown grass.

She took a deep calming breath and slid from the car, gingerly walking towards the house. Thorns from wild, untended bushes crunched under her feet and she turned with wide eyes to watch Jim following with her case.

'I know this is a shock for you,' he said apologetically, 'but it wasn't something I could tell you about. You have to see it for yourself.' Taking a deep breath, he stepped past her on to a shallow porch and pushed open the front door.

No one was about and everything was silent and still when she followed him into the house. An uncarpeted living room with a high ceiling met her guarded gaze, and suddenly she shivered. It was deserted, forsaken. A lampshade was tipped drunkenly on a broken lamp and everything was powdered with a heavy greyish film of dust. The cushions of a sofa were nothing more than a jumbled mass of foam rubber stuffing spilling out from split seams. There must have been several years' accumulated dirt here and even a wide stone fireplace was full of dead white ashes.

An overpowering, musty odour came to her, but she swiftly quelled the wild impulse to turn around and leave. 'People actually live like this?' she whispered.

Jim's face was grim. 'Live? Richard sleeps here sometimes, and Charlotte comes and goes without much supervision. A hired hand cooks the meals in the kitchen, but I doubt if anyone's set foot in this room ever since the night Peter Talbot died.'

Her eyes opened even wider. 'Peter Talbot?'

'Richard's father. Didn't I mention him? He was a good man, fair in a lot of ways. His only flaw was he was afraid of getting old.' Jim's brow furrowed as if he was remembering something unpleasant. 'I warned him not to marry a woman so much younger than he was—she'd be the death of him. But he wouldn't listen. Now he's dead and Richard's left with all this.'

'This isn't Richard's house?'

'It wasn't. His stays here were temporary after he graduated from university. He moved back for good when he brought Susan home from the hospital three years ago.'

Megan's bewildered gaze swept around the room again. 'Does he expect her to rest easy in a mess like this?'

'Oh, Susan's room is altogether different. It's outfitted with the most expensive equipment he could find. He spares no expense when it comes to her care.' Raking an impatient hand through his hair, Jim sighed in exasperation, trying not to stir up the dust as he walked through it. 'But for all that, he refuses to see her. Do you know, for the last three years he hasn't set foot in her room once? I don't know why. I used to think he blamed himself for her illness in some way. But I've told him more than once we don't know where it comes from, why some people are stricken and not others. I've tried to get him to talk about it, but he won't.'

She shivered again but didn't say anything.

Jim led her through a short hallway to the back of the house. 'We usually use the back door, but you had to see what you're up against,' he explained.

The kitchen was almost as bad. She walked to the round table in the middle of the big room and looked all around with wide frightened eyes. A rank musty smell choked her. 'Oh, Jim!' she whispered.

The wooden cabinets on two walls were filthy with grime and hung open to reveal the chaos inside. There were dirty dishes in a large rusty sink and the floor was gritty underfoot. In one corner, an ancient stove was caked with a greasy film of dirt and a refrigerator, equally ancient, stood forlornly next to it. A large window over the sink was covered with a filthy dark green curtain, blocking out the warmth of the sun, and she shuddered and impulsively straightened the grimy green oilcloth on the table.

'I know how you must feel,' said Jim, coming close to her and taking one of her small cold hands in his. 'I should have prepared you for this, but I didn't know how. If you think it'll be too much for you . . .'

She lifted her chin and a look of resolution began to replace the dismay in her eyes. Not for anything in the world would she let him see how much of a shock this was to her. Somehow she had just never pictured Richard Talbot living in a place like this. 'I haven't seen your patient yet,' she said softly. 'She's all that really matters, isn't she?'

Jim sighed and started towards a door on the far side of the kitchen, when he stopped abruptly, seeing Richard coming up the overgrown path to the back door with tired, dragging steps. His jeans were covered with mud and his arms were dirty where his shirt sleeves had been rolled back to the elbows. When he came into the room, he didn't see them.

For a fleeting moment Megan's stomach somersaulted as she looked at him, seeing his rich black hair falling in an unruly mass across his forehead when he took off his stained felt hat and ran a tired hand across his eyes. Her senses started to swim and a burning warmth flooded her body and an almost wanton impulse tingled all through her, drawing her towards him like a magnet. Yet she stood still, her lips parting involuntarily, her breathing quickening as she kept drinking in his nearness.

Oh, God, she prayed, not having the slightest idea what she was praying for.

An hour could have passed, standing, looking at him like this, or a minute. The only thing she was certain of was that she was here where she belonged. It was as if she had come home.

Sensing another presence, Richard looked up and saw her through the gloom, and stiffened. Jim was the first to break the silence.

'Hello, Richard.'

He immediately straightened and his features hardened into sharp cold lines. 'Jim,' he said, barely nodding in their direction.

'I told you she'd come!' Jim's voice held a note of barely concealed triumph.

'No sense crowing about it. She won't be staying very long.'

'That's where you're wrong,' said Megan quickly, trying to cover the hiss of her sharply indrawn breath. 'Now that I'm here, I have every intention of staying.'

Those incredibly blue eyes, diamond-hard, swept an insult over her. 'You won't last a day.'

She wasn't the least taken aback. She had come home, and nothing would make her leave. 'Would you care to bet on that?'

His black eyebrows rose and his disbelieving gaze sliced to Jim, but Jim merely shrugged and tried not to look as if he was enjoying himself. 'Are you obstinate, Megan? Or just plain pigheaded?' demanded Richard.

'I prefer to call it "determined",' she said sweetly.

'God help us all!' With that, Richard turned on his heel and walked out of the door, slamming it hard.

A stunned second later, she found her voice. 'Well, that seemed to shake him up, didn't it?'

Jim sighed. 'It'll probably be a whole lot easier on you if you just try to ignore him. I don't think he means to be rude. It's just that he's a driven man.'

'I'm not afraid of him,' she said determinedly. 'But I think he wants me to be.'

He stared at her for a minute, then his expression softened. 'There's something here scaring all the other help away. It's a comfort to know that if it's Richard, at least you won't let him get to you. Come on, we might as well meet your next hurdle.'

When Megan stepped through a small connecting doorway, it was hard to believe she was in the same house. Jim wasn't kidding when he had told her Susan's room was different. It was a suite, really, with two large airy bedrooms and a small bathroom. The walls were a soft pastel blue with frothy white eyelet curtains at the wide windows to give an impression of coolness. Everything was incredibly clean and quiet and thick ice blue carpeting muffled their footsteps.

'Jim?' A tiny thread of a voice drew them to the high metal hospital bed.

'Hello, Susan. How are you feeling today?'

Susan Shea was lifted high on pillows and her breathing was laboured. Dark, pain-glazed eyes flared briefly when she spotted Megan, but she managed to nod in her direction. 'Will the pain ever go away?' she sighed.

'The new medication didn't help?' asked Jim.

'I can't stand it any more, Jim.'

A frown creased his forehead when he turned to the small table next to the bed and opened the chart lying there. 'It says here you slept through the night. I consider that a little progress.'

'Progress! I'll consider it progress when I stop hurting!'

He took her blood pressure and checked her reflexes and looked into her eyes. 'Let's continue with this medication a few more days and give it a chance to take hold,' he said with a firm but gentle bedside manner. 'I've brought you a new nurse—Megan Crane. Try not to be too hard on her, will you?'

'Megan?' Susan said coldly, her dark eyes snapping, all trace of pain vanishing. 'Why can't Jeanne stay? I'm used to her.'

'Sorry, Susan, I need Jeanne at the office. You've been running through nurses at such a rate, my bookwork is backlogged at least six months.'

She smiled maliciously, running a hand through her short dark hair prematurely streaked with white. 'Wouldn't it be easier to find a replacement for your office than to keep looking for nurses for me?' she asked.

'You know that's impossible. And you've got to remember, Jeanne's been with me for a long time. Why, she practically runs the hospital by herself! If you want me to keep coming out here as often as I do, who do you think will mind the store while I'm gone?'

'Don't be difficult, Jim!' snapped Susan.

'I can be as difficult as you, my dear,' he said with a grin.

'Megan, eh?' She flashed a look of dislike in her direction. 'Well? Haven't you anything to say for yourself?'

'Miss Shea.' She came forward, nodding

seriously, forcing herself to remember that this
broken woman had once been used to having the
world at her feet. 'It's an honour to meet you.'

Susan's eyes were piercing as she searched
Megan's face for some sign of insincerity. When
she couldn't find any, she actually preened.
'You've seen my films, then?'

'Oh yes, every one.'

'And what did you think?'

'You should have won an Oscar several times
over.'

'I should have, shouldn't I?' She lifted a
graceful hand to her forehead. 'The pain is
getting quite bad, Jim. Isn't it time for my
medication?'

He consulted her chart and looked up when a
plump elderly woman came from the smaller
bedroom with a suitcase in her hand.

'Not till dinner, Susan,' she said firmly in a low
pleasant voice. 'The pills have to be taken with
meals, remember?' Then she beamed a smile at Jim
and held out her hand to Megan. 'You must be
Megan Crane. Jim rang me last night and said he
thought you'd come. I'm Jeanne Drummond.'

Megan liked her at once. Her handshake was
warm and firm and capable. Motherly, she
thought, smiling back at her.

'Come along, I'll show you where I keep the
medication.' She tucked Megan's hand in the
crook of her arm and led her to a small locked
cabinet on the other side of the room. 'I've made a
list of the things Susan needs done for her and the
times and so forth. Look at it and tell me if there's
anything you don't understand.'

Megan scanned the paper, then looked directly
into the nurse's twinkling eyes. 'How much of this

is an act and how much is real?' Her voice was low enough not to reach Susan.

'Ah!' Jeanne Drummond's smile was wide. 'She's such a good actress she makes you wonder, doesn't she? Her pain is real, though, and there are some days when she finds breathing difficult. Her chest muscles sometimes give her problems. Just be firm with her, and gentle, if you can. My phone number's there if you need me.'

She turned and motioned to Jim that she was ready to leave. 'Try not to be too hard on this poor girl, will you, Susan?' she said quietly, patting her hand before stepping towards the door.

'I'll be back to see you soon,' smiled Jim. 'Megan will walk us to the door and come back with your dinner.'

'Goodbye, Jim,' Susan sighed theatrically. 'Your visit is the only thing that brightens my day.'

He smiled and motioned for Megan to follow them to the kitchen. 'So far, so good. Do you think you can handle her?'

She had seen nothing as yet that had scared off all the other nurses. 'I'll try, Jim.'

'That's all I ask of you.'

She looked past him and saw a tall, blond young man about eighteen years old turning away from the stove, coming towards her with a tray in his hands. Surprisingly, there was a spotless white towel covering it.

Jim turned and introduced them. 'Megan, this is Franz Schmidt, Richard's hired hand. Franz, Megan Crane.'

'Ma'am,' he nodded absently before handing her the tray. It was obvious he had been introduced to many different nurses in the past and didn't consider her any different from the rest.

'Mr Schmidt,' she said, looking with disconcerting directness into his clear blue eyes.

Taken aback, he stared at her. 'Mr Schmidt is my father. Everybody calls me Franz.'

'Franz, then.' She smiled up at him and was rewarded with a reluctant white flash of teeth in his darkly suntanned face.

'I have a tray ready each morning at seven, twelve-thirty and again at six,' he said awkwardly before nodding and making a swift exit.

'Thank you, Franz,' she called after him.

Jim grinned and shook his head. 'He was always so shy before—I never heard him say more than two words at a time! How do you do it, Megan?'

She smiled serenely, not letting him see the sudden surge of panic threatening to grip her now that he was actually leaving. There were a lot of sensations beginning to crowd in on her and she couldn't sort them out yet. What if she wasn't equal to the task? 'I won't disappoint you,' she said, more for her own benefit than his.

'Remember, I'm just a phone call away if you need me.'

'I'll remember.'

Megan wasn't prepared for the violent change that came over Susan when she brought the tray in to her.

'He's out there, isn't he?' she sneered.

Megan's head jerked up in surprise. 'Who?'

'Don't play innocent with me, Miss red hair and green eyes and all that milky white skin. You can eat your heart out with wanting him, but he's mine!'

Megan stared at her with rounded eyes.

'Answer me!' Susan shouted. 'He's out there, isn't he?'

'I don't know who you mean.'

'Such phony innocence!' Her face twisted. 'Richard's mine! You can't have him, do you hear? Every nurse that comes here tries to make a play for him, but it won't work. He's mine—he'll always be mine. I won't let him go!'

'I wouldn't expect you to,' Megan said soothingly, trying to gain time to figure out what to do to calm her down. She'd never come across jealousy like this before, and so unfounded, it totally threw her.

'You think you're very clever, don't you?' sneered Susan.

'Not at all, Miss Shea.' She kept her face blank. Maybe the best thing to do would be to act normally. She quietly went about arranging her tray at the side of the bed. It was a pleasant surprise to see the fine china and smell a tantalising aroma drifting up to her.

But Susan caught her off guard and before she could stop her, she picked up a cup of bubbling hot chicken broth and dumped it in Megan's face.

It stung and burned and dripped from her hair down her nose and on to her blouse. Scrubbing at her eyes, she fell back, but managed to move the tray out of Susan's reach before she could do any more damage.

'That's just a taste of what you'll get if you dare to stay here!' Susan screamed shrilly.

'I'm not leaving,' choked Megan, trying to hold her blouse away from her burning skin. 'But thanks for the warning.'

It took her a good ten minutes in the bathroom to wash the broth from her hair and flush her reddened skin with cold water. Changing into more comfortable clothes, she fought to regain her equilibrium before she again approached the bed.

Susan's eyes were closed and she looked as if she was sleeping, but Megan wasn't taking any chances.

'Where are you going with that tray?' she cried when she saw Megan pick it up and start towards the door.

Megan stiffened but didn't turn around. 'I'm taking it back to the kitchen.'

'But I haven't had my dinner yet!'

'Oh?' She glanced back over her shoulder. 'I was under the impression you didn't want it.'

'Bring it back!'

'Not on your life, Miss Shea—I'm not that stupid. We'll try again at breakfast.'

Megan walked out and all she could hear through the heavy door were muffled curses. 'That's one for me, she thought with a heavy smile. Then she froze. Richard was sitting at the kitchen table waiting for her, a certain smugness twisting his lips.

'You knew!' she accused him, her heart thumping.

'I told you you wouldn't last a day,' he said. 'From the looks of you, she threw the soup.'

She was astounded by his calm acceptance of his wife's behaviour and an unaccustomed rage swept through her. 'The least you could have done was warn me!' she snapped.

'You're lucky it was only the soup,' he told her. 'With the last one, it was a knife.'

Megan was aghast. 'Does Jim know?'

'No, he doesn't. And I'd appreciate it if you didn't tell him either.'

'So that's why all the other nurses left and never
said anything.' She stared hard at him. 'Somebody
should tell him. It's wrong to keep it secret.'

'And what would that accomplish except to
have him dope her up and keep her semi-conscious
all the time?' Richard rose to his feet and stood
towering over her.

His impassive face only ignited her anger.
'Don't you realise how dangerous she is?'

'Jealousy is a dangerous emotion,' he shrugged.

Her mouth dropped open at his deliberately
indifferent tone. Her temper seethed and she
stepped to the grimy countertop and set the tray
down with a thump, trying to crush the rebellion
swelling inside her. 'Then why don't you go in
there and tell her she has nothing to be jealous of?
Jim told me you haven't set foot in her room in
three years.' She was overstepping herself, but the
tight control she had kept on her emotions since
coming here suddenly broke and her eyes blazed at
him. 'Don't you know what that's doing to her?'

'Mind your own business!' he grated, the
muscles in his jaw leaping savagely, his eyes
flashing like hard blue stones. 'Get your suitcase. I
have to go into town anyway, I'll take you back.'

Squaring her shoulders, Megan faced him
without moving. She wanted to shriek at him, but
forced herself to a freezing calmness. 'I'm not
leaving.'

'Even after what she did to you?' His black
eyebrows rose in haughty disbelief.

'Especially after what she did to me.'

'You're a fool!'

'Maybe so,' she said with a sudden shiver of
apprehension. 'But I told you before, I'm staying.'

Richard's strong mouth thinned and his eyes

wandered up and down her curving figure, lingering pointedly on her full, rounded breasts.

Her face flamed at the insult and her chest felt so tight she couldn't breathe, but she stood absolutely still, stubbornly refusing to let him see how much he unnerved her. He brought out the worst in her and she knew later she would have to get down on her knees in penance for reacting this way, but she just couldn't help it. He didn't want her here, and that was all she needed to make her stay.

'Of all the obstinate, bull-headed——' he muttered harshly. 'I've tried to make it plain I don't want you here.' He clamped his jaw so tightly shut there was a trace of white at the sides of his mouth. 'If anything happens to you, I won't be responsible.' Savage blue eyes searched her face for long measured seconds before he pivoted away from her and slammed the back door behind him.

The breath she had been holding whistled when she expelled it. In spite of his blazing antagonism, for one fleeting moment she had glimpsed a searing pain in his eyes, and it caught her and held and she thought, absurdly, he was trying to force her to leave for her own protection.

Her eyes widened and she stared ahead blindly. Protect her? From whom? His wife? Or—himself?

CHAPTER FOUR

IT was a full minute before Megan noticed the little girl standing by the stove watching her. Stiffening, she could only guess how long she'd been there. Somehow she managed to smile and keep her voice even. 'Hello,' she said.

Without answering, she came forward and through the gloom Megan could see she was a spindly little girl about eight years old. She was barefoot and her fists were bunched in a faded cotton blouse hanging shapelessly over jeans much too small for her. Her hair was twisted in a long dark braid almost to her waist. She didn't say anything, but Megan was caught by her eyes. They were even bluer than Richard's.

'You must be Charlotte,' she said gently, taking a step closer to her.

The girl's eyes widened and stayed riveted on her as she jerked back away and pushed her hands into her back pockets, thrusting her chin forward. 'My name's Charley.'

In spite of the belligerence in her voice, Megan detected a faint uncertainty. 'I'm glad to meet you, Charley. I'm Megan.'

'Are you really staying?' the child asked, giving her a long, fierce look.

'Didn't you hear me tell your dad that?'

'I bet you didn't really mean it.'

'Yes, I do.' There was a slight shake of her head as Megan turned back towards Susan's room. 'Both you and your dad don't want to believe me, but you'll just have to see for yourselves.'

During the next twenty-four hours, Megan became even more determined to stay, if only to prove to the whole Talbot family that she was a lot tougher than she looked.

Susan resorted to hurling her pillows when she realised Megan had moved everything else out of reach. Megan retaliated by refusing to give them back.

'But I'm in pain!' she shouted. 'I can't breathe when I lie flat!'

'You should have thought of that before you threw them at me.'

Her calm low voice only infuriated Susan more. 'I'll ring Jim and tell him you're mistreating me and you won't give me anything to eat!'

'Go ahead. The phone's right over there.' Megan pointed to a small glass-topped table beneath the windows on the other side of the room.

'You know I can't get out of bed. Ring him and tell him I want to see him immediately!'

'I've already talked to him once today and told him everything was fine and he didn't need to make a trip out here. Oh no, I'm not calling him again. If you've got any complaints, you'll have to call him yourself or else wait until he comes.'

'Oh, I hate you!' Susan spat before hurling a long string of abusive curses at her.

Half the words she used Megan had never heard before and, mercifully, had no idea what they meant. The half she did understand made her gasp, but she kept her face blank and her voice quiet.

'You can keep on with this tantrum you're

throwing or you can have lunch. Which is it going
to be? If you don't want it, tell me and I'll take it
back to the kitchen.'

Susan's fists curled and Megan knew she longed
to get her hands on the tray and throw the whole
thing at her, but she had already missed two meals
because of it and she didn't think she'd be stupid
enough to keep this up much longer.

'If I eat my lunch instead of throwing it at you,
will you give me back my pillows?'

Megan gave her a long measured look before
stepping close to her and expertly slipping three
pillows behind her back. 'Now for the tray,' she
murmured.

For an instant their eyes met and clashed and
Megan stood poised, ready to whisk it away if
Susan so much as moved.

'You took the knife,' Susan said coldly. 'How
am I supposed to cut this fish without it?'

'I've already cut it into bite-size pieces for you.'

'I'm surprised you let me have a fork.' Heavy
sarcasm twisted the other woman's face.

'If you don't want to eat with your fingers from
now on, you'll get rid of the idea of planting it in
my back,' said Megan sweetly.

'You think you're very clever, don't you?'

Megan sighed. There was no room for cleverness
here; it was more like a basic instinct for survival.
'Not at all. I'm just trying to keep one step ahead
of you.'

Susan's shoulders shook with amusement and
she tackled her lunch with relish. When she had
finished, she sank back on her pillows and let
Megan take the tray without trying anything.
'What do you think of Richard?' she asked, a look
of innocent curiosity on her lined face.

Megan was instantly on guard. 'I really don't know anything about him,' she said truthfully. As far as she was concerned, Richard was a taboo subject. The less said about him, the better.

'Do you think he's handsome?' Susan persisted.

Knowing her volatile jealousy, Megan chose her answer carefully. 'Those eyes of his are striking, but Charley's are even more so.'

'You've met the little urchin, then?'

Megan was surprised that Susan took no motherly pride in her daughter, but she supposed her jealousy extended itself to her too. She gave her her medication and again tried to be tactful. 'Charley seems a plain little thing now, but maybe she'll grow up to be a beautiful woman.'

'Not if Richard has his way,' said Susan, yawning. 'He wanted a son instead of a daughter. It was an obsession with him. Haven't you noticed? That's why he calls her Charley instead of Charlotte.'

Megan digested this in silence, not quite knowing what she was driving at. She wasn't left in doubt long.

'So if you think you can get to him through her, forget it!' shrieked Susan. 'He's going to realise how wrong he is to stay away and come in here and see me and let me forgive him.' Her eyes filled with pathetic tears. 'But I've got to get rid of you first. He'll never want me if he has you.'

'Please,' Megan's voice was low and steady in an effort to calm her down, 'try to rest now. Let your medication work. I assure you, I have no interest in your husband.'

'My hus——?' Susan broke off, frowning. Then suddenly she became more agitated, shrieking wildly. 'He *is* my husband! Do you hear me? He *is*.

He's all I ever wanted. Peter wasn't half the man his son is. I never loved Peter. I tried, but there was only Richard—only Richard!'

Megan couldn't make any sense out of her ravings and tried to reassure her again. 'Would it help if I told you I intend to become a nun some day?' she said helplessly.

Susan stopped dead, lifting her head and staring at Megan's white face. 'You? A nun? With your face and figure?'

The sound of her rough mocking laughter sent icy chills up and down Megan's spine and it echoed in her mind long after Susan had finally subsided into a deep drugged sleep.

'I will become a nun,' she told herself over and over. 'Richard means nothing to me. I won't let him mean anything.'

Finishing her own lunch, she stood at Susan's bedside for long minutes listening to her laborious breathing. Considering her restless night, she knew Susan would sleep the rest of the afternoon. So she took the time to telephone several art galleries to let them know her change of address and her continuing hope of finding her paintings.

An hour passed and she became more and more restless, knowing it was a dim hope but refusing to admit it. Her paintings were some-where, she just knew it; she could feel it in her bones. Her arm brushed against the tray of soiled dishes, and she suddenly found the perfect way to cure her restlessness. Quickly changing into an old paint-stained pair of jeans and a T-shirt, she purposefully made her way to the gloomy kitchen.

Charlotte was there at the table, staring into space, her chin resting on her cupped hands.

Looking up at Megan searchingly, it was a long minute before she spoke. 'You're still here?'

'I told you I was staying,' Megan said gently.

'My dad says you're not really tough. You're just out to prove something.'

'Maybe he's right.' Megan's chin lifted a fraction. 'Would you like to help me with these dishes?'

'You don't have to do them. Franz usually takes them all to his mother's house after supper.'

Megan looked at the pile in the sink and grimaced. 'I'd imagine he's got other, more important things to do. There ought to be a dishpan and soap around here somewhere.'

At this prospect of doing something different, Charlotte got up without any hesitation and helped to look for them under the sink.

'It might help if we let some sun in here so we can see what we're doing,' said Megan, reaching up to the window. The dark green rag came away in shreds, letting the sunlight filter through the streaked glass. 'There, isn't that an improvement already?'

An awkward silence fell as they both looked at all the dirt and then looked at each other with wide eyes.

Charlotte started to laugh and that broke the ice and for the rest of the afternoon she was a most willing helper. She chattered away, telling Megan how much she hated school, loved her father, and how she regarded Franz almost as an older brother. She mentioned Susan only once, by her stage name, which Megan thought was odd, and that was to say that she was too young to really remember her as anything but an invalid.

When the dishes were dried, they unearthed an

old broom and a bucket and a scrubbing brush,
and after several hours, they began to see a
difference.

Charlotte couldn't contain her surprise. 'Gosh!
It looks like a real kitchen again!'

Megan grinned tiredly, squatting on her heels on
the floor in front of the cabinet she had just
finished cleaning, her water-wrinkled fingers
smoothing the thick slippery weight of her hair out
of her eyes.

'We did a lot of work, didn't we?' Charlotte's
little face glowed with a sense of accomplishment.
'It looks so different now.'

The porcelain finish on the sink and stove and
refrigerator was a gleaming white again and the
curtainless window over the sink and on the back
door shone.

'I never knew the countertop was white,'
Charlotte laughed, coming to sit on the floor
beside Megan with her knees drawn up to her
chin.

'It just goes to show you what a little soap and
water and a lot of elbow grease can do.' Megan's
eyes danced. 'All that's left is the floor, but Susan
was beginning to stir the last time I looked in on
her, so it'll have to wait.'

She started to push herself up when the back
door slammed and a thunderous voice split the air.

'What in the hell——?'

'Daddy!' Charlotte scrambled to her feet,
knocking Megan off balance, sending her sprawling on her back on the grimy floor.

Before she could get up, Richard stood towering
over her, his long legs astride, hands on hips, a
look of murderous rage twisting his face. 'What's
going on here?' he shouted.

If he meant to put her at a disadvantage, this was the perfect way to do it. She felt like a fool lying here at his feet. 'We were house-cleaning.'

'Why?' His anger slashed at her, holding her motionless, letting his icy blue eyes look deep inside her.

'Because it needed it,' she dared to whisper back.

That infuriated him even more. He swooped down and roughly lifted her to her feet, then let her go at once as if he couldn't bear to touch her. She stumbled forward, her hands automatically shooting out to keep her balance. His shirt was unbuttoned and when she touched the muscled skin of his sweat-stained chest, her heart lurched crazily in her throat.

She would have fallen, but his hands roughly caught her waist to steady her, somehow pulling her against the entire length of his long heated body. For a startled breathless second, all she could do was stare up at him. She'd never been this close to a man before, and her mind stumbled all over itself with strange new sensations.

Clamped against his hard unyielding muscles, she was dwarfed by the sheer strength and power emanating from him. And that power was there, too, in the granite stillness of his face, in those bitter blue eyes slashing down at her, and in the angry tightening of his mouth.

Then all at once the mask of his anger slipped, the bitterness faded, changed, became something else. His magnetism tingled through her and her heart began to pound in thick suffocating strokes. She felt his breath stirring her hair, now a wild tangle of red fire about her face. With one big hand splayed wide against her back and the other low on her waist, he was all lean hard muscle quivering warmly against her.

His bright blue gaze swept over her face as if memorising each feature, leaving a trail of heat on her skin, cutting off her already shallow breathing. Everything around them receded. They could have been the only two people in the world, so complete was their absorption with each other. Richard must have murmured something, because she saw the firm line of his mouth move, but with her heart pounding so maddeningly fast in her ears, she couldn't hear or understand what it was. For the life of her, she couldn't move. Her eyes were fixed on him, catching a sudden glimpse of something—something. She couldn't define it, but she knew instinctively it was forbidden. Her lips were slightly parted, her eyes huge and glazed and brilliantly green, her hands unknowingly curling, digging into the rapid rise and fall of his chest.

'Megan?' Charlotte tugged at her trouser leg. 'Why is your face all funny?'

Startled by the tiny voice floating up to her, Megan blinked and Richard's arms fell away to his sides. She stepped back on unsteady legs, gasping a little, her heart still hammering in her throat. Her face felt flushed, but her eyes couldn't leave his. 'Charlotte?' She heard her voice as if from a distance and it was unrecognisable, so thick and husky and breathless.

Richard turned to his daughter and his eyes narrowed as his face settled back into its familiar harsh lines. 'Why aren't you at Mrs Schmidt's? Franz said he saw you walking that way this morning.'

'I wanted to stay home today, Daddy,' she said guiltily, stepping a little closer to Megan as if for protection. 'To see if Megan really was staying like she said.'

'Well, if she is staying, it's not for your benefit,' he said callously. 'She's here to care for Susan.' His suddenly ruthless gaze slashed back to her. 'She should be more than enough to keep you busy.'

'She's been sleeping since lunchtime.' Megan swallowed, forcing herself to meet his angry look without quivering. 'I'm not neglecting her.'

'I've never known her to sleep during the day before,' he said coldly.

'She had a very restless night last night. She's probably just making up for it this afternoon.'

'Did you give her the right dosage of medication?'

His attitude was one of accusation and she bristled in self-defence. 'If you're implying that I purposely drugged her, you're wrong. 'I wouldn't do such a thing.'

'Why not?' he sneered, his face cold and bitter. 'It wouldn't be the first time someone's tried it. With that foul mouth of hers, it's a wonder no one's given her a lethal overdose yet!'

Megan caught her breath in a startled gasp. Maybe he had no illusions about his wife, but surely he should watch what he said in front of Charlotte?

His mouth tightened. 'I won't have her drugged. If it's too much for you, just say so and I'll take you back.'

'That won't be necessary.' She breathed in deeply and squared her shoulders. 'I told you before, I'm staying.'

'Then stay where you belong! I don't need a Miss Do-Good meddling out here.' His powerful arm made a sweeping arc to encompass not only the kitchen but also the rest of the house. 'You won't be paid extra to clean my house for me.'

She felt her jaw start to drop. 'I never expected to get paid for it,' she said in a strangled voice. 'Charlotte and I did it simply because it needed to be done!' She glared at him for a tense second and nodded curtly to Charlotte, then quickly walked away before she said something she'd regret.

That night it was she who was too restless to sleep. She was still angry at Richard's reaction to the clean kitchen, yet she supposed she could understand it too, once she really thought about it. He didn't want his wife neglected. As she paced her bedroom floor, her thoughts whirled. She was keyed up, every nerve in her body throbbing. Even the quiet beauty of the dark, moon-silvered vineyard in the distance outside her window didn't soothe her.

She wasn't sure what was happening to her. All she knew was that during those few moments in Richard's arms, she had been caught by something totally new and alien and she could only stand helplessly, remembering, as it swept through her. Even now, after she had fed and bathed and settled Susan for the night, it wouldn't leave her. Nor would the memory of the changing expression in Richard's eyes. It was there, vividly clear, but she was too inexperienced to know what it meant.

Stumbling to the bathroom, she plunged her hands into ice-cold water, splashing it in her face in an effort to rid herself of this memory and the strange, uncontrollable stirrings in her body. Gasping, she looked in the mirror, expecting to see someone different looking back.

'You're a fool,' she whispered to her burning reflection. 'A stupid naïve fool. Mother Superior was right—you need to face reality and stop letting your imagination run wild. Nothing happened. Nothing's different from the way it was yesterday. Nothing's changed.'

She allowed herself only a moment to wonder what Richard might have thought, but the sense of humiliation became too painful. Whatever happened, or didn't happen, in that moment had to be hidden, buried, forgotten. If nothing else, he was a married man. She wouldn't let herself forget that again. And she wanted only to become a nun.

Jim came two days later with her mail, which had no news of her paintings. When he walked her back to the kitchen after checking on Susan, he let out a troubled breath. 'You've worked a miracle here,' he said softly. 'But I don't understand how. How did you ever find the time? You're managing Susan beautifully, and still you're able to make a change in here too.'

Richard's voice, harsh and cutting, intruded from the back door. 'It's easy, Jim. All you have to do is overdose the patient so she sleeps all the time.'

Megan stiffened before turning to face him. She hadn't seen him for two days and had forgotten how arrogant and callous he could be. 'I did no such thing!' Her eyes swivelled back to Jim. 'It's all here on the chart, how much medication and at what times.'

'Don't you believe it, Jim.'

Jim searched Megan's face then looked at Richard coming towards them. 'Are you calling her a liar?'

'Doesn't it seem strange to you that everyone

else failed with Susan, but along comes this little slip of a thing and she manages without a hitch?'

'Why do you resent me so much?' She rounded on him, looking straight into his burning eyes. 'Is it because I proved you wrong?'

'You've only been here three days. That's no big accomplishment.'

'But you said I wouldn't last one!'

Jim stood back in surprise and watched the two of them strike sparks off each other.

'So what do you expect? A medal?' Richard's lip curled in a sneer.

'I don't expect anything from you, but I won't have you accuse me of neglect. I did not give Susan anything other than what's on that chart.'

Jim cleared his throat before holding it out to him. 'It all seems to be in order here. And I trust Megan. If you want to have a look at it——'

'Then why is she sleeping so much?' Richard waved the chart away with an impatient hand. 'You know I don't want her drugged.'

'It's one of the side effects, I suppose. I can lessen the dosage, but I really think the rest is doing her good. I'd rather leave it for the time being.'

'No.' He was adamant. 'I want her awake—and aware.'

'But you don't know how unbearable her pain can be.'

Richard's eyes became curiously bleak and bitter. 'Don't I, Jim? Don't I?'

After a moment, a long sigh came from somewhere deep inside the doctor. 'All right, I'll lessen the dosage.' He wrote swiftly on the chart, then looked at Megan. 'Half a tablet twice a day. Call me if you need me.'

'Oh, she won't,' said Richard with heavy sarcasm. 'She's out to prove something.'

Megan lifted her chin, her green eyes flashing. He was so hateful, always waiting for her to admit it was too much for her. She could do nothing but respond. 'Do you think I can't?' she demanded.

Jim frowned at both of them standing there so taut and still, facing each other with open antagonism. He rubbed a thoughtful hand over his chin before a reluctant smile tugged at the corners of his mouth. 'Well, anyway, I'll be back at the end of the week if I don't hear from you sooner.'

But he didn't come then. He was called out of town, and Jerry Nolan came in his place and brought Lora with him.

Megan hadn't realised how much she had missed her until she walked Jerry to the kitchen and saw her waiting for them. 'Lora!' A bright smile lit up her face.

'Are you all right, Megan?' asked Lora. 'This job's not too much for you?'

'Not at all,' she smiled. 'Susan isn't hard to handle as long as I'm firm and stay one step ahead of her.' Her smile became rueful. 'And I have lots of time to write letters to all the galleries and supply houses. I still haven't abandoned my hope there.'

'Well, that's a relief,' Lora sighed. 'For a while there, I felt so guilty. After all, it was partly my fault you came out here. If I hadn't introduced you to Richard ...' She pulled out a chair at the table and motioned for her to sit down. Quiet speculation was in her eyes before she swung a look to Jerry.

'You're sure you've had no trouble with her?' he

asked quietly, finishing his notes in Susan's chart. 'I've heard certain rumours.'

'No, Jerry. You might say Susan and I—understand one another.'

Lora chewed her bottom lip and her eyes were troubled. 'Are you sure? You look as if you're losing weight to me.'

'You're imagining things, honestly,' laughed Megan. Her clothes didn't fit quite as snugly as before, but it wouldn't hurt her to lose a few pounds. 'You don't know what great cooks Franz and his mother are.'

But that didn't satisfy Lora. 'You say that, Megan, but you look different somehow. You're not finding it too isolated? I know you didn't go out much when you lived in town, but at least then you spent some time at art stores and talked to people. Here there's nothing but rows and rows of grapevines.' She wrinkled her nose.

'I haven't really had time to feel isolated,' Megan said with some surprise. 'And I don't know if I'd ever feel that way if I lived here for years. It's such beautiful country, and Charlotte and I talk in the afternoons sometimes. And Franz has been telling me about his family whenever he gets a few minutes away from his chores. Do you know, his family dates back to the 1850's when the first Germans settled here? His father is a sixth generation German wine-grower. And Franz is the youngest of ten children.'

Lora was diverted, but Jerry wasn't. 'That's all very well and good, but what about Susan?' A wry smile twisted his face. 'I always heard she was impossible to handle. Look at the way she refused to let me examine her.'

'That's only because you're so young and good-

looking.' Megan chuckled softly and flashed a
look at Lora. 'I've found that as long as her
husband isn't mentioned, she's controllable, but
once his name comes into the conversation, she
gets wild.'

'Still? But it's been three years since——' Lora
broke off and shuddered delicately.

Megan guessed they had tried to talk Richard
into seeing Susan and had suffered the same fate
she had. She shrugged. 'I've found it best to
change the subject, but it's not easy. She manages
to twist everything back to him.'

'Poor Megan.' Lora was all sympathy. 'I don't
think I could stay here like you do.'

'It's my stubborn streak, I suppose.'

'You haven't had any time off yet. Why don't
you talk to Jim about it when he gets back? It
would do you good to get away for a couple of
hours. You could come to town and we could have
lunch.'

'I don't think——' began Megan—only to have
the words die in her throat when she saw Richard
in the doorway. He was leaning against one side
with his arms folded across his chest and a
maddening smile on his handsome face. From his
relaxed attitude, he had been standing there quite
some time.

'What's the matter, Megan? Afraid once you
leave here, you won't have the courage to come
back?' He looked straight into her eyes with a half
mocking smile.

Her chin went up in an unconscious gesture of
challenge. She hadn't seen him for the past three
days and all it took was one look at him again and
all her carefully built defences crumbled. She was
irresistibly drawn to him. 'Courage?' she said, her

eyes still fixed on him. 'No, I don't need courage. No matter where I went, I'd always come back. I know how much you need me.'

'Need!' he thundered, jerking away from the wall, his whole powerful body stiffening. 'You're the last person in the world I need!'

Lora's jaw dropped. Jerry's face showed an equal surprise, but he was quick to recover his composure.

'Er—would you mind walking Lora to the car, Megan?' He came between them quietly. 'I'd like to have a word with Richard about Susan's medication.'

'Of course.' She tore her eyes away from Richard and forced a smile, resolutely turning her back on a pair of harsh, icy blue eyes seething with rage.

When they stopped at the side of Jerry's station wagon, Lora's face was a study in awestruck wonder. 'Megan! Why did you say such a thing to him?'

She sighed raggedly. 'I don't know why. There's something about him . . . He resented me coming here at first, then somehow it became a challenge to see if I'd stay. Now I suppose it's just a battle of wills to see who admits defeat first.' Her eyes flickered with a sudden look of shame. 'I've got to stay, Lora. Maybe it's wrong, but I don't want to leave here.' She pressed her fingers to her mouth as if to keep back the words. 'Susan rambles on a lot and there are so many things I don't understand. I wish I could have met Peter Talbot. She talks about him so often, but then her jealousy takes over and she loses control. She keeps accusing me of all sorts of unspeakable things with her husband.'

'But you never even knew him!'

'Try telling her that. Richard could settle everything if only he'd see her, but he won't. I have this horrible feeling he enjoys listening to her ravings.'

Lora's eyes widened even more.

'And then there's Charlotte,' Megan went on. 'She's such a sweet little thing, yet she has to listen to the most awful language I've ever heard.'

'Megan!' Lora breathed. 'This is no place for you. Jim told me about you—and the convent. Come home with me now. We stopped at Jim's office and picked up your mail. Maybe there's a letter that says your paintings have turned up.'

'I doubt it,' said Megan softly, squeezing her friend's hand. 'Somehow it doesn't matter any more. I just want to stay here. It's more than just caring for a bedridden patient and trying to prove to her family I can do it. Something's keeping me here.'

'Please, Megan!' shuddered Lora. 'The way you say that gives me the creeps!'

A desperate little laugh came from her. 'It's nothing like that. Maybe I just feel needed for the first time in my life. Everything's going to work out all right—I just know it.'

CHAPTER FIVE

THE weeks slipped by and the dry summer days lengthened, bathing the vineyards in a golden glowing sunshine. Megan settled into a comfortable routine, and one day a week Jeanne Drummond cared for Susan while Megan usually spent the day in Adelaide, trudging from one out-of-the-way place to another. She followed up every lead, no matter how slight, always hoping to stumble across her paintings. They were gone, lost to her, and she knew it. But she wouldn't give up. Sometimes she took Charlotte with her and sometimes she went alone, but always she returned to the Talbot house with a fresh sense of homecoming.

She loved this sprawling, rolling open country with its fragrant green vines climbing the sloping hills and spent many afternoons quietly sketching the scene from her window. She rarely saw Richard, and then only fleetingly, from a distance.

'The vines are green now,' Susan murmured from her bed, watching Megan's fingers fly across the sketchpad one sultry afternoon, 'but they'll soon turn gold and vermilion and bronze and deep purple—like the colours of wine.'

Megan looked up and surprise flashed in her eyes. 'Why, that's almost poetic, Susan!'

'You look surprised. Didn't you think I had it in me?'

'Oh, no—that is—I mean——' Megan stumbled all over herself trying to cover up the unthinking blunder.

'You're just like Peter.' Susan's face twisted. 'He never thought I was capable of an original thought either. It was always Christina with him. To listen to him, you'd think no one else could appreciate poetry or music or art. You'd think she was his w——' her voice broke off abruptly and she pressed her lips together as if wishing she hadn't said anything.

'Who's Christina?' Megan asked quietly.

'Er—it doesn't matter. She's dead now. She died the same day Peter did.'

'Oh. I'm sorry.'

'Don't be,' Susan said spitefully. 'She's better off dead.'

Megan's eyes widened and she looked taken aback.

'Er—she was in a car accident,' Susan said nervously, pulling at the ribbons on the front of her white nightgown. 'She would have been a cripple if she had lived.'

'Oh. Well, I suppose some people would rather not have to face that.' Megan watched Susan's reactions without making it obvious. An unmistakable tension suddenly vibrated all around her. Megan felt it but couldn't understand it. Whoever Christina was, she had the power to reduce Susan to a trembling mass of nerves. 'Was she Peter Talbot's wife?' she asked with a frown.

Susan blanched. 'What makes you say that?'

Megan shrugged her shoulders. 'When I first came here, I remember Jim saying something about Peter marrying a woman much younger than himself. I just thought, from the way you coupled them together, she might have been his wife.'

Relief washed over Susan's face. 'Yes. Yes, that's it. Christina was Peter Talbot's wife.'

Megan didn't pursue it, hoping this wasn't a prelude to another one of her jealous tantrums. Whenever she started talking about Richard's father, the conversation eventually led to Richard, and then she lost all reason.

But it was a vain hope, she realised less than an hour later. Susan was more and more restless and petulant, no matter how Megan tried to pacify her.

'It's been a long time since Jeanne was here,' she muttered, her face drawn, her words slurring. 'I want you to read that book she started last week.'

Embarrassment washed over Megan. 'But Susan, I can't read that!'

When Susan saw the quick rise of colour in Megan's face, she shrieked wildly, 'Dammit—it's not *that* indecent! Everything else has been taken away from me. At least let me hear about somebody else's wild love life. Just think of it as only some author's words on paper.'

'But such words!' Megan's mouth clamped shut in a tight thin line. 'People don't really *do* those things, do they?'

'Where have you been all your life?' Susan accused shrilly, her voice bouncing around the room. For several minutes she struggled to regain her breath. 'You're how old? Twenty-five?'

'Twenty-four.'

'And an innocent virgin to boot? Come off it, Megan. No one's a virgin at twenty-four in this day and age.'

'I told you, I'm going to be a nun.'

'And my nervous system's going to clear up and let me walk again!' Susan sneered sarcastically. 'If

you believe either of those things, you're a fool.
Get off the nun kick—you're not fooling anybody.
You can't tell me a girl with your looks and your
body has never known a man.'

'I haven't,' Megan said unsteadily. It was almost
an apology. 'I grew up in a convent.'

'I can't believe you're for real! Haven't you ever
wondered what it might be like to be loved by a
man?' Susan's voice suddenly softened to a
whisper and Megan found herself drawing close to
Susan, listening breathlessly, somehow finding
herself in the picture she was describing. '. . . to be
held fast in his powerful arms with a gentle
roughness you've never known before.' She spoke
slowly, in a seductive husky voice, watching
Megan's reaction out of the corner of her eye. 'To
be moulded to his solid, warm, lean length and feel
his trembling desire. To have his hands loosen
your hair and thread his quivering fingers through
its flaming thickness before lifting your face gently
to his, his lips moving back and forth, gently,
sensuously, on yours in a burning kiss . . .'

Susan barely breathed the name—Richard—but
Megan saw him clearly in her mind, and in that
split second she let down her guard and gave
Susan the advantage.

Her hair had fallen out of its loose coil and,
standing as close to the bed as she was, Susan was
able to grab a thick handful. She viciously jerked
Megan's head back before scoring her nails down
one side of her face.

'He's mine!' she rasped. 'You'll never have him!'

Megan cried out, feeling the stinging spurt of
blood on her cheek. Trying to grab her hand away
from her head, she could only capture one of
them. The other was tightly wound in her hair,

holding her still, keeping her face close to the twisted insanity of hers.

'Please, Susan,' she pleaded frantically, raw pain filling her voice. Her eyes were wide with shock. 'I'd never touch your husband.'

'He *is* my husband,' Susan insisted, her face twisted with jealousy. 'He is. He always will be.'

'I don't believe in divorce,' Megan cried. 'Even if he tried to leave you, he'd still be married in God's eyes. You don't have to worry that I'd take him away from you.'

'He won't divorce me,' Susan laughed hysterically. 'He can't! But he's mine—he'll always be mine.' Her fingers tightened, curling into vicious claws. 'If you try to take him, it'll kill me. Do you want that on your conscience, *nun*?'

'No,' whispered Megan, swallowing her desperation. If she could only get her talking normally, maybe she could escape. There had to be some way. Her hand was trying to pry Susan's fingers loose from her hair, but her grip was iron hard. She searched for some sign of sanity in Susan's demented face as she tried to ease away from her.

'If I die,' Susan's grin was unnerving, her dark eyes curiously empty and glazed, 'I'll have more of a hold on him than ever. You'll never be free of me. I'll always come between you.'

The smouldering light in her eyes should have warned Megan, but before she could brace herself, her hair was viciously yanked again and her cheek crushed against the cold metal railing of the hospital bed. Shock threw her off balance. Before she could regain it, she fell heavily to the floor with Susan's hand still twisted tightly in her hair.

Susan tried to pull her back up, but she didn't

have the strength.

Megan was fast losing consciousness. Swirling hot pain ripped through her skull. All she could feel was her head bobbing back and forth and terrible crushing blows to her temple where her head was banging against the side of the bed. All she could hear was Susan's wild insane laughter and the words, 'I'll never let him go!' echoing round and round until a merciful, empty black void opened up and swallowed her.

Then all at once she felt blissfully safe, warmly cradled against a solid wall, yet strangely floating. Her mind refused to probe the sensation too deeply for fear it would stop and that horrible pain would begin again.

I must be dead, she thought, trying to open her eyes to see where she was. She heard a deep gentle murmur close to her face and felt a fierce tightening at her sides when her lashes weakly fluttered open.

'I didn't think heaven would be blue,' she said, full of wonder, staring straight into two round pools of burning cobalt. 'As blue as Richard's eyes,' she murmured. 'I could drown in them.'

All at once a blackness swam before her and a fine sweat stood out on her forehead. She felt something cold pressed against her lips before it trickled down her chin and on to her dress. A crushing wave of black pain surged through her. A deafening roar sounded in her ears and she swallowed convulsively at the thick bile rising in her throat.

Then, somehow, she knew she wasn't dead. Richard was there and she was cradled in his arms. Her head was firmly pressed against the hard wall of his chest and she could hear a deep erratic

booming. Long bluish-white grooves slashed the
sides of his mouth when she blinked up at him.

'Richard?' she murmured, completely caught by
his strangely shimmering blue eyes. 'It wasn't
heaven at all. It was you, wasn't it?'

When his face came closer to hers, she didn't
think it strange. She met the soft whisper of his
breath against her lips before her mind started to
reel into an endless shining oblivion.

When Megan woke, she blinked and lay perfectly
still, staring at the morning sunlight dancing on
a cobwebby ceiling. She could hear crickets
chirping in the distance. A slight breeze came
through the open window, bringing the soft
soothing murmur of birdsong. She was in a
room she had never seen before, in a big bed
with a thin cover over her. A chest of drawers
and a night table and a small straight-backed
chair were covered with a fine layer of dust, but
nothing was out of place. Dirty oak flooring was
partially covered by a carpet disappearing under
the bed. When she tried to turn her head, a
stabbing pain made her gasp and suddenly
everything came rushing back.

'Are you all right?' The tiny voice beside her was
a mere thread.

'Charlotte?' She blinked rapidly to bring her
into focus. 'Where am I?'

'You're in Daddy's room.'

'How——?' She closed her eyes and waited for a
spasm of pain to recede.

'You didn't come for Susan's tray,' Charlotte
said quickly, her fingers straying to Megan's cold
hand lying flaccid on the thin blanket. 'I told
Franz there must be something wrong. He went to

Susan's room and found you and . . . and . . . I ran for Daddy.' Her eyes filled with tears.

'Don't cry, Charlotte. It's all right,' Megan said softly, linking her fingers with her tiny hand.

'Oh, Megan, we thought you were dead! Doctor Crawford was going to get an ambulance, but Daddy had already carried you up here and he wouldn't let you be moved. Are you sure you're all right? Your face is almost as white as that bandage on it!'

Megan's fingers curiously bumped along a thick soft square on her cheek. 'I'll be fine. I'm just a little tired, that's all.'

'I better go tell Daddy you're awake. He's been staying here with you, but Franz needed him for something, so he told me to let him know if you woke up.'

'How long have I been here?' asked Megan before Charlotte reached the door.

'Three days.'

When Megan opened her eyes again, Richard was seated in the chair close to the side of the bed, his head bent. Her hand was being crushed in his and for a long moment she stared at the silky black thickness of his hair. Such magnetism, she thought desperately, her senses racing as he lifted his head to look at her. Even now, after all this, he reduced her to a trembling mass of nerves and emotions and wanton desire.

He looked haggard and worn with several days' growth of beard stubbling the hard angle of his jaw. His deep blue eyes were bleary and shot with faint red lines. 'This never should have happened,' he said harshly.

Flinching, Megan flushed a deep red. She was such a fool. She had built him up in her mind, but she meant nothing to him. He hadn't wanted her here in the first place. He even warned her. If he knew how she was drawn to him, it would only embarrass him. 'I'm sorry, I—I—it was my own fault. There's no excuse I can give you.'

He stared at her for a pulsing second before his expression became cold and grim. 'That's not what I meant.' He released her hand and a groan came from somewhere deep inside his chest as he got to his feet. Both his hands clutched the back of his neck and he stared at the ceiling. 'You told me she was dangerous, but I never realised she'd go that far. After all this time, I thought . . .' He levelled his piercing gaze at her again. 'She almost killed you.'

'I don't think she really meant to.' The tightness in her chest was stifling.

He loomed above her in seething anger, his eyes narrowing, his molten blue gaze moving over each feature. 'Look at you! You're scratched and bruised and swollen. You've been knocked senseless for days. And you can lie there and say she wouldn't have killed you if she could have got out of bed and finished it?'

'She's a sick woman and I'm not really a nurse. I didn't know how to handle her.' A bitter sense of failure came welling up. 'But I had to prove something, didn't I? I was wrong. I shouldn't have been too stubborn to admit it.'

He straightened up and turned away before letting out a harsh sigh, his expression becoming cold and dispassionate. 'Jim should be here soon. We'll see what can be done about moving you.'

Megan lifted her chin proudly on the pillow, fighting off a swift stab of self-pity. 'Of course— I'll leave at once. I'm sorry I caused you all this trouble.'

Richard's lips twisted, but he didn't look at her. 'Thank you for staying as long as you did. Naturally, I'll pay for all the medical care you'll require.'

Suppressing a shiver, she stared at the ceiling. Bright sparkling tears stung her eyes, but she kept her voice even. This was the end of everything, but she still had her pride. 'That won't be necessary,' she said quietly.

'I don't blame you for not wanting anything more to do with me, but I insist. Susan did this to you and I'm responsible for it.'

'No! It was my own stupidity.' Her colour receded when she remembered what Susan had been saying just before the attack. Her eyes squeezed shut, but she could still see his face, the glinting blue eyes with the fine crinkling lines at the corners from squinting in the hot sun, the strong uncompromising jaw and cleft chin tanned to a golden bronze, his curling black hair, thick and unruly. To imagine herself loving him was to sink to the depths of depravity. He was a married man and she was going to be a nun. Hating herself, she turned her face into the pillow and wished with all her might that she had never come here.

When she surfaced again, Jim was there. A deep worried frown etched his face as he stood looking down at her.

'How's my patient?' he asked.

'I'm sorry, Jim. You didn't need another one,' she apologised.

'But you are, so we'll just have to make the best of it.' His smile was warm, his touch gentle. 'Do you think you can sit up?' He put his arm under her shoulders and lifted her to a sitting position, slipping several pillows behind her. 'How does that feel?'

When the room stopped spinning, she was able to give him a tremulous smile. 'I think I'm going to live.'

'Would you care to tell me what happened?'

She started to shake her head, but it throbbed. 'No,' she said softly. 'Susan's a jealous woman. There's nothing more to say.'

'Yes, there is,' muttered Jim. 'I thought you were going to be honest with me. Richard finally told me—everything.'

Megan bent her head. 'About why all the other nurses wouldn't stay?'

'Yes. He was wrong to ask you to keep it from me, to expose you to that kind of danger.'

'He was only trying to protect her. He didn't want you to keep her doped up,' she breathed huskily.

'Oh God! Is that what he told you?' He pounded his fist into his other hand. 'Such innocence! To you, everything is all sweetness and light, isn't it? He was punishing her, Megan. He wanted her to suffer.'

'No!' She didn't want to believe that. Not Richard. He wouldn't do such a thing. Ice slithered down her spine. She kept shaking her head. 'No—I don't believe it.'

'Believe it, Megan. He blamed her for Christina's—and Peter's—death, so he was making her pay. That's why he never would see her, why he kept himself so tantalisingly out of reach. To make her suffer!' At her wince of pain, he gritted his teeth. 'I was wrong to involve you in this. If only I'd known! I never should have asked you to come. I've got to get you away.'

She turned vacant eyes away from him, not wanting to believe him. Oh, Richard, Richard—his name echoed in her mind. 'So where do I go from here?' she murmured unsteadily.

'First of all we've got to get you better.' Jim's mouth twisted and he bunched his hands in the pockets of his dark slacks. 'I'd take you home with me, but my wife's in Sydney, visiting her mother for six weeks, so there'd be no one to stay with you during the day while I'm at the hospital. Lora said you could come to her, but her landlady isn't the most understanding person in the world, is she? Even if you could get a chance to explain.'

Megan grimaced. 'I think Mrs Simpson would love to tell me "I told you so".'

He turned to the window, looking out to the vineyards glowing in the sunshine. 'You're not sick enough to take up a hospital bed, even though Richard said he'd take care of the cost.'

'No!' She asserted her independence with a painful lift of her chin. 'I'm not his problem. And I don't want you sending any bills to him for my care, either. I'll pay you myself.'

His expression thundered. 'A certain amount of stubborn pride is all well and good, but isn't that what got you into this—mess—in the first place?'

She backed down then and looked at her hands twisting nervously in her lap. 'I hate to have to admit I failed.'

'You didn't fail! I told you that. You lasted longer than any of the others.'

'Richard waited every day. He knew I'd have to ask him to take me away from here and I—I just couldn't!' She buried her face in her hands and to her ignominy, started to cry.

'Oh, Megan.' Jim sat on the bed next to her and

watched helplessly. 'Go ahead, cry it all out. Sometimes it's the best medicine in the world.' He put his arms around her and turned her face into his chest and sat for a long time listening to her hiccuping sobs.

When she finally lifted her head, he brushed away her tears with a crisp white handkerchief and handed it to her. 'You've got your bandage all wet,' he said gently. 'I'll have to change the dressing to keep the stitches dry.'

'Stitches?'

He nodded and reached for his black bag on the table beside the bed. 'Eight of them. You're going to have a scar, I'm afraid. But I hope I'm skilled enough that it'll be a thin one.'

When he removed the tear-soaked bandage, the loud hiss of an indrawn breath turned them both to the doorway.

'Come in, Richard,' Jim said coldly. 'Take a look at Susan's handiwork.'

As he stood rigid, Richard's hands were knotted into fists at his sides. He was wearing faded Levi's and a long-sleeved blue and white checked shirt and for a second he looked carved from stone. His stride was stiff and hesitant as he came closer. Diamond-bright eyes swept over her, noting her red-rimmed eyes in her pale face, her hair tumbling down her back in deep red waves, the thin straps of her white cotton nightgown. They glittered with something she didn't understand when they settled on the angry red streaks on her cheek.

Jim was still sitting on the side of the bed close to her. 'Hand me the tape, will you, Richard?' Folding a gauze square, he gently covered the wound.

Without a word, Richard cut several strips and handed them to him.

'There's no infection, so we can be thankful for small favours,' Jim said quietly, getting to his feet.

Richard's face was impassive and although she knew she was staring, she couldn't take her eyes off him. Broad muscles rippled beneath his shirt as he knotted his hands at his sides. Raw power seemed to flow from him, suffocating her and she shivered with undeniable yearning. If only she had the right to throw herself into his arms and beg him to hold her and wipe away the horror she had been through. She was sure she'd find more than the solace Jim had offered her. But no. She silently struggled with herself. No—it was absurd to feel this way. She had to get over it now. He was a man with no morals, a man who delighted in punishing his wife. Given half a chance, what would he do with an innocent like her?

'Have you decided when she can leave?' Richard asked shortly.

'She should be able to get out of bed in an hour or so and walk as far as the bathroom, but she's not going anywhere for the next few days.' Jim looked at her and smiled gently. 'By that time I should be able to find a place for you to stay.'

Richard's eyes slashed to her and narrowed accusingly. 'Aren't you going back to New York where you came from? To your family? Friends?'

Megan's heart pounded wildly and her chin shot up. No way was she going to let him see how hopelessly alone she was. 'It's not your worry. I'll——'

'Jim?' He cut her off with a slicing look.

'She doesn't have a family,' he sighed. 'No friends who could keep her either. But there may be one of the girls at the hospital who's looking for a roommate or someone to share expenses.' He smiled again and gripped her shoulder reassuringly. 'I'll start asking this afternoon and get back to you as soon as I can.'

'That won't be necessary.' Richard's voice was cold, his expression granite hard and just as unyielding. 'She'll stay here until she's well again. This is my responsibility.'

'No!' she gasped. 'It was my own fault.' If he meant to silence her with the burning anger of his look, she disappointed him. 'You told me that first day you wouldn't be responsible if anything happened to me.'

'I said you'll stay.' He turned to Jim and gave him a long measured look. 'You've got enough to do with your patients. Leave Megan to me. I don't want to hear any more about it.' He turned on his heel and left them both staring, open-mouthed, after him.

CHAPTER SIX

THAT night, when Megan came back from the bathroom, she kept her hand lightly on the wall for balance. A small table was somewhere near and she didn't want to bump into it and disturb anyone. The darkness was so complete she couldn't see her hand in front of her face, but, unerringly, her toes found the table leg. Her sudden gasp of pain brought a bright, blinding light to the narrow hallway.

'Are you all right?' Richard was standing barefoot close to her with his hand on the light switch. A pair of jeans was all he wore and for a breathless moment she felt the warmth from his body before her eyes nervously skittered away from all that smooth tanned skin.

A brilliant wash of colour ran up her neck and into her face. 'I—I'm sorry, I didn't mean to disturb you.' She stood on one bare foot in embarrassment, conscious of her thin nightgown. From the sudden darkening of his eyes, she knew it didn't conceal much. Averting her head, she started past him, wincing at the sudden pain splintering through her foot when she stood on it.

'What's wrong?' he asked.

'I stubbed my toes,' she said miserably, trying to swallow past the pulse racing in her throat.

An exasperated sigh reached her ears. 'That usually happens when you can't see where you're going. Why didn't you turn on the light?'

'I didn't want to wake anyone.'

'Charley sleeps like a log. A light wouldn't have bothered her.'

'But I bothered you, didn't I?' Her innocent eyes widened when she lifted them up to his and met the deep burning blue.

'I wasn't asleep,' he said. 'I heard you go into the bathroom.'

Her swift shallow breathing became strangling and her stomach contracted nervously. 'I'm sorry, I should have realised you couldn't rest. I've put you out of your room—I'm in your bed——'

Dark red blood congested his face and his hands closed over her shoulders, paralysing her with his touch. 'You know just what to say, don't you? Yet you can stand here and look so damned innocent!'

'I—I don't know what you mean.' Her eyes looked straight into his and skittered away at once, only to be caught by the firm sensual line of his mouth. Even if she wanted to, she couldn't look away from it. For one blind instant that terrible yearning overwhelmed her again. She watched his lips part and move with disturbing sensuality and caught a glimpse of his even white teeth.

'You know exactly what I mean,' he said thickly, one hand curving around the back of her head, his thumb fiercely tracing her jawline. 'It's there in your eyes. Why pretend?'

She felt herself irresistibly pulled against him and was powerless to stop the motion. In an unhurried movement, his other hand slid behind her back, stroking the warm softness of her body through her thin nightgown.

'Megan,' he muttered, his face twisted. 'Megan.'

With a muffled groan his mouth found hers with

an urgency that sent the blood roaring in her ears. All her senses were inflamed as his mouth covered hers, coaxing hers open, exploring, teasing, filling her with the taste and scent and feel of his powerful masculinity. His hands roamed surely down her spine, caressing her, arousing sensations she didn't know existed. Her untutored body quivered in reaction to the hard male frame throbbing against hers. It was a devastating awakening of emotions she had never before experienced, and her hands fluttered helplessly before timidly settling on the warm pulsing muscles in his back.

Her hesitant touch seemed to inflame him even more and he gathered her even closer, crushing her, threading his fingers through her flaming hair. 'Dear God!' he murmured unevenly. 'I never thought I could feel this way again.'

It was just as Susan said it would be, she thought, held in his arms with a fierce rough gentleness she had never known before. And then she stopped abruptly, dragging her mouth away from his, trying to twist her boneless body out of his arms. Susan! How could she forget his wife? Worse, how could he?

'What is it?' he asked in a strangled voice. 'Am I hurting you?'

'Please, Richard,' she pleaded, stiffening her arms against his chest when he tried to keep her close.

'Please what? Please go on? Please make love to me? You want this as much as I do—I can feel what your body is telling me.'

Her heart hammered wildly when he swept her off her feet and turned towards his room. She was held easily against his burning warmth, and when the light clicked off, she had the disorientated sensation of falling yet being held fast and safe. Then she felt the coolness of sheets against her back and a sudden erupting fear strangled her chest.

'Shhh,' he whispered. 'I won't disappoint you.'

For a screaming instant she stiffened. Shock held her rigid until she felt his hands gently caressing her shoulders before sliding under the thin straps of her nightgown to pull them down. His lips brushed against hers, softly tantalising, before becoming hard and hungry and seeking. His breath was warm when his mouth left hers to follow the path his hands made to the swelling roundness of her breasts.

'No!' She thought she shouted, but her voice came out in a choked whispered cry. 'Don't! Please, I've . . . never . . .' She shuddered convulsively and sudden thick tears of shame and humiliation spurted down her face.

Stiffening, Richard leaned over her, reaching out to switch on a small lamp at the side of the bed and peering down at her stricken face. One of his hands was at the side of her head, caught in the dark red tangle of her hair. 'I don't believe it,' he said harshly.

She couldn't look at him and turned her face away, filled with shame, trying to drag her nightgown over her nakedness.

'You're nothing but a damned tease!'

Megan's eyes squeezed tightly shut. There was nothing she could say. Everything that had happened between them was beyond her comprehension. She could only feel—and be staggered by those feelings.

His voice thickened with fury. His fingers

gripped her chin and roughly forced her face back to his. 'Why the sudden change of heart? Don't I measure up to all the others?'

'Others?'

With a sound of disgust, Richard pushed himself to his feet and stood towering beside her. 'Why so coy?' he mocked. 'You've given me just enough to whet my appetite. You've got me all tied up in knots so I can't think straight. But it's all a business with you, isn't it?' He gritted his teeth. 'All right, how much?'

Too confused to grasp his meaning, Megan stared at him, her eyes huge and bewildered. And then it dawned on her what he was asking. 'Oh God!' she choked. 'Get out of here! Go! I hope I never have to see you again!'

His shoulders sagged in defeat. 'All right, Megan, I'll go. But I'll be back. We'll see how long it takes before you beg me to come back to my bed where I belong.' His eyes burned through her. 'We'll see what your price is then.'

For a week Megan refused to come out of the tiny bedroom at the end of the hall. She had moved her things out of Richard's room at once and refused to budge from there. Jim was puzzled, and whenever he questioned her, she would colour painfully and keep her eyes trained on the tall bitter man bent over his vines outside her window. So many times he would stop what he was doing and just stand there, looking at the house as if he knew she was watching him. Then he would gently run his long fingers over the ripening fruit in a caressing motion, mocking her.

Each time she saw him do that, she could feel again the tantalising touch of his hands, his mouth, on her breasts, and wanted to die of shame.

'If you don't tell me what's bothering you, how can I help?' said Jim harshly, abandoning all pretence of a bedside manner. 'You look worse now than you did the first night Richard brought you up here. Why did you move out of that room and into this one? It's so dreary in comparison.'

Megan mumbled something he couldn't hear and kept her head down.

'Why are you hiding up here away from everybody? Franz says you don't eat and Charlotte hasn't seen you for days.'

'I'm not hiding.' She bit her lip, staring at her hands on the windowsill, hating herself for lying to him.

'I'm a doctor, Megan. I know when someone's malingering. Your headaches should be gone by now and your cheek is healing nicely.'

She thrust her chin up. 'It's not that.' Her voice broke and it took several minutes to regain her composure. 'I just can't face him again.'

'Him?' Jim stopped abruptly and stared at her before he let out a harsh breath. 'By "him" I suppose you mean Richard?'

She nodded miserably. 'Oh, Jim, what am I going to do? I know I shouldn't stay here, but God help me, I don't want to leave.'

Gently taking her hands in his, he made her look at him. 'I don't know what might be between you and Richard, and I'm not asking you to tell me. But I can tell you this—whatever it is, it's making him change. You're exerting some kind of influence already. Look at the way he's abandoned his petty plan of revenge against Susan. He actually admitted he was ashamed of himself for wanting to hurt her more than she already has been hurt. Would you believe it? A man as arrogant as he is?' His face softened. 'Don't think about leaving yet. You might be the one who'll finally bring Richard all the way back to the man he was before Susan became a blight on his life.'

'Oh, please! You don't know what you're saying.'

He sighed and shook her gently, struggling to keep the exasperation out of his voice. 'I can't tell you what to do, I can only suggest. You have to work things out your own way. But come downstairs while you're doing it. It's almost teatime. Don't you think Franz could use some help?'

A look of resignation crossed her face before she took a deep breath and squared her shoulders. 'I'm beginning to look ridiculous, aren't I?'

'No, not really. But it's time to go on. Whatever differences you have with Richard will work themselves out. In spite of his harsh ways, he's a good man. I'd trust him with my life.'

It wasn't that she didn't trust Richard. It was herself, her own reaction to him, she couldn't trust. 'Do I look all right?' She nervously brushed her hands down the sides of her blue gingham sundress.

His smile turned to a grin. 'I've found when a woman starts to worry if she looks all right, she's almost cured. Get some meat back on those bones,' he chuckled, 'and you'll look like the beautiful girl I first brought here.'

Luckily, Richard was nowhere around when they came downstairs. Charlotte was at the table, straddling a chair backwards, and Franz had his back to her, looking at a cookbook open on the counter. In just this short time, the kitchen was beginning to take on an air of neglect again; dirty dishes were piled in the sink and the floor was more gritty than ever.

'Hello, Charlotte, Franz,' she said softly, unconsciously bracing herself.

'Megan!' Franz's bright eyes danced and an irrepressible grin changed his whole solemn face when he looked over his shoulder. 'Welcome back. You're feeling better?'

Curiously relieved, she let out her breath and nodded, returning a small shy smile before turning to Charlotte. 'Charlotte? I missed you——'

'My name's Charley!' The little girl's whole manner was decidedly hostile, her face twisted with hurt. 'Don't ever call me Charlotte!'

Everything inside Megan froze.

'That's enough, young lady,' Franz said harshly, turning from the sink.

'I'm not a young lady!' She jumped to her feet. 'I'll never be a lady—they're nothing but trouble!' Megan glimpsed the shimmer of tears before the back door slammed behind her.

Jim let out a long slow breath. 'I thought she was over that. Richard too,' he added as an afterthought. 'But Franz, here, appreciates a good woman. Don't you, my friend?'

Franz spoke firmly. 'I'll take care of Megan. You don't have to worry.'

Jim nodded and picked up his bag before extending his hand towards him and then to Megan. 'Jeanne's with Susan. We told her you went back to New York, so don't go near her. If you feel up to helping Franz, fine. Otherwise, just get plenty of rest and fresh air. That's all the medicine you'll need.'

'I'll feed her well,' said Franz with a twinkle in his eye. 'You won't recognise her the next time you come!'

When Jim had gone, Franz caught her troubled glance and smiled in reassurance. 'I'm glad you decided to stay on with us for a while.'

'There was no place else for me to go.' Flushing, she realised how ungrateful that sounded. 'I'm sorry, I didn't mean it that way.'

'All things happen for a reason, don't they?' he said gently. 'Even something like this?' He reached out and lightly brushed her cheek. 'If it wasn't for this, you might be gone now and Richard would still be locked in his bitter despair. You've helped him already. Wait till he gets to know you more.'

Megan grimaced and sat down in the chair Charlotte had vacated. 'He doesn't want to know me, Franz. And he's still a very bitter man, though I don't know why. I'm the trouble Charlotte was talking about. You must have realised that?'

'Try to forgive him,' urged Franz. 'He only thinks he hates all women, but he doesn't really. It's only been since Susan . . .'

In spite of herself, she couldn't bite back her sarcasm. 'I'll bet it was long before that. You're letting your loyalty colour his faults.'

'Perhaps. My family owe him and his father a lot.'

At her look of interest, Franz pulled out a chair and sat at the table with her. 'You have to try to understand. The year before I was born was a very bad year for the grapes. There was a drought and my family would have lost everything, but Peter Talbot loaned us enough money to keep us afloat. He didn't have to do that; he had enough troubles of his own, being a widower with a fourteen-year-

old son. But he took a fancy to my mother and
father and treated our family as an extension of his
own.' A faint remembering smile curved his
mouth. 'When each of my brothers and sisters
married, he gave them an acre of adjoining
vineyards as a wedding present.'

'He doesn't sound like the same man Susan
talked about.'

'No, well, when he married again, everything
began to change.' His mouth twisted. 'He became
silent and withdrawn. My father said he was
disillusioned, but my mother said it was just
because she was so much younger and he didn't
know how to cope with her artistic temperament.
But then Richard came home from college to help
with the failing vineyards and he brought new life
to this place and to his father. It looked as if
everything was going to work out again. Charlotte
was a tiny baby then and Richard was so full of
love and laughter.'

Megan frowned. It almost sounded—but how
could that be? Susan said Richard was her
husband, not Peter.

Franz went on and cut that thought short.
'Susan was the only fly in the ointment.' He
shrugged expressively. 'She was restless and bored
and jealous. Peter's attention wasn't enough for
her; she had to have all of Richard's as well, but he
was spending more and more time away from the
house doing the things he loved best: tending the
vines, almost mothering the grapes, experimenting
with new varieties and hybrids. Susan resented it.
She resented everything Richard had, everything
he did. Eventually she came between him and
Christina and his father.'

'Are you saying Chri——'

'That's enough gossiping, Franz!' Richard came in the back door and silently closed it behind him. His face was cold and hard and he looked as if he was having difficulty controlling himself. 'I'm sure Megan isn't interested in the past history of the Talbot family.'

Franz stepped back to the stove and his colour deepened at the reprimand, but he didn't say anything.

'I asked him,' she said in a low voice that shook, her eyes not quite meeting his.

'If you have any questions concerning me, ask me. Or are you the type who'd rather listen to distorted gossip?' His lip curled.

Megan flushed painfully, but stood up and forced herself to face him. 'I was trying to understand why Charlotte resents being a girl.'

'She'd have been better off a boy.'

'But she isn't! Why are you trying to make her deny it?'

'Women are nothing but trouble,' shrugged Franz. 'You'd have to be a man to understand that.'

'But I'm not.'

His glittering blue gaze swept over her, stopping insultingly on the ripe roundness of her breasts beneath the blue gingham. 'No, you're definitely not a man, are you?' Megan knew he was remembering the fiasco of five nights ago.

She tried to ignore the sudden wild pounding of her heart before turning abruptly away, biting her tongue to keep from saying something she'd regret. She reached in the cupboard for the plates and silently began to set the table with awkward jerky movements.

Dinner that evening wasn't a pleasant meal.

They waited quite a while before Richard found Charlotte hiding in a low gnarled apple tree in the back yard. Her mutinous scowl every time anyone looked at her did nothing to help their digestion. Franz's manner was strained too, although he quietly moved about the kitchen with all the efficiency of a first class waiter.

Megan should have been hungry, but when she looked at the chunky vegetables steaming in the plate of lamb casserole in front of her, she felt her stomach churn and kept trying to swallow. Her mouth felt dry and full of cotton. She managed to pick at the food, crumbling a piece of thick homemade bread while trying to make a pretence of enjoying it, but she kept feeling Richard's eyes on her. If only he'd finish his meal and leave, maybe then she could relax and force something down.

But when he finished, he pushed his plate aside and stared relentlessly at her white face across from him. 'Is there something wrong with your dinner?' he asked, barely concealing his impatience.

She looked up and swallowed convulsively, wishing the roaring in her ears would stop. 'Not— at all.' She breathed deeply. 'I just don't seem to be hungry right now. Oh!' To her ignominy, she stood up with a jerk and ran out of the room with her hand over her mouth.

How she made it to the bathroom without retching all over the stairway was a miracle. Putting a dazed hand to her eyes, she finally stood up weakly before a cold towel was gently pressed to her face. Someone must have told Jeanne Drummond, she thought, and closed her eyes and relaxed, letting the capable hands take care of her.

'Feeling better?' said a deep mocking voice.

She stiffened and tried to turn away, but Richard merely bent over the wash basin and rinsed the cloth again in cold water. His expression was full of detached indifference, but her face flamed and she felt hot and cold at the same time and filled with unbearable humiliation.

'I thought Jim had a talk with you about stubborn pride? Why didn't you say something instead of sitting there, trying to act as if nothing was wrong?' One big capable hand spanned the back of her head, holding her still, while the other sponged her burning face. 'Hold still!' His tone was harsh now.

She couldn't help shuddering. She had never felt so humiliated in all her life. 'If you knew I was going to be sick, why did you just sit there watching me?'

'I wanted to see how far you'd go.'

'Now you know!' she lashed out bitterly.

'You're a fool, Megan,' he told her.

She stood stiffly, her head bent in shame. 'You told me that before.'

Releasing a slow angry breath, Richard stood away from the bathroom door and gave her a long, level look. 'Go to your room and lie down. I'll have Franz make up a tray.'

'I can't put him to that trouble,' she argued.

'You are trouble, Megan. Nothing can change that.'

Her head came up at once, antagonism flashing in her stricken eyes. 'Then why did you insist that I stay here?'

'Where else would you go?'

'I'd call Jim——'

'His wife's out of town for the next month or

so—you know that, I heard him tell you. Are you so frustrated you'd pick on a married man old enough to be your father?'

Her hand struck his face.

'What's the matter, Megan? Does the truth hurt?' He didn't move. A bright red handprint stood out on his cheek, but he made no move to touch it. 'If you ever do that again,' he said softly, 'you'll be in for an unpleasant shock. In this age of Women's Lib, men have the option to hit back. I'm a lot bigger than you. One swing and——' He lifted his shoulders and left the threat in the air between them.

'Don't you ever make such an accusation again!' Her face was completely white, but she stood her ground, bristling with anger.

An unwilling smile played at the corners of his mouth. 'You never back down from me, do you? You try to argue with Jim, but in the end you always let him have the last word.' His brilliant eyes narrowed, skimming over her before stopping on her trembling lips. 'Why not me?'

He took a step closer, but she backed away until she was brought up sharply against the bathroom wall. 'Please, Richard,' she whispered.

'Such big green eyes, and so full of invitation,' he mocked, coming even closer. 'I love to hear you beg.'

'I'm not—begging.'

'You're always saying, "Please, Richard".' His voice was a mere breath, his lips an inch away but not yet touching hers. 'I want to hear you say it again. "Please, Richard".'

'No!'

'Why?' Are you afraid of me?' His whisper was closer.

'No,' she breathed. 'I'm afraid of me!' The minute she said it, she could have bitten out her tongue.

'Ah,' he said softly, satisfaction making him straighten away from her but leaving both hands on the wall at the sides of her head. 'How could you make such an admission?' His eyes roamed over her again, narrowing to diamond pinpoints. 'You certainly know your business well. You must command a very high price. How many men have been willing to pay it?'

Megan blinked bewilderedly, not knowing what he was talking about.

'When you look at me like that, you seem so innocent,' he mused. 'I could swear you're untouched.'

A brilliant red surged up her neck and he laughed. 'How do you do that? Does it have something to do with your red hair?'

'Please, R——' She put a hand to her mouth and choked back the words, turning her head away, pressing herself flatter against the wall. Her legs were trembling so badly she thought she'd fall.

A laugh rumbled deep and mockingly in his throat. 'Go lie down before you fall down.' He gave her a little shove in the direction of her room. 'Go,' he muttered, 'before I lose my temper.'

Colouring hotly, Megan fled.

When Richard came back with a tray she was standing by the grimy window looking out over the rapidly darkening countryside. 'You're supposed to be lying down,' he grumbled.

She shrugged awkwardly. The last place she wanted to be was in bed if he was around. But was that true? some devil inside her mocked. Wouldn't she love to spend the next several hours right there with him? Disturbing images ran through her mind and she stood there helplessly. This was madness. Oh, what was there about him that drew her so strongly?

He brushed past her with a scornful look, ignoring her colourless face, and set the tray on the nightstand beside the bed with a thump. He drew up a dusty wooden chair for her to sit on. 'I want you to eat all of this,' he said irritably, pointing to a soft-boiled egg, two slices of toast and a cup of strong, honey-sweetened tea. 'It isn't all that much, but it won't be heavy on your stomach. Franz tells me you haven't eaten in days.' He waited. 'Well, go on. Eat!' He turned his back and stood looking out of the same grimy window where she had been standing only moments before.

Her face burned. Didn't he know he wasn't helping by staying here? Oh, please go, she begged silently.

She choked down part of the egg before he came to sit on the edge of the bed. 'Thank you,' she said stiffly. 'I'm sorry to have troubled y——'

'I said eat it all!'

Her cup clattered on the saucer, but he ignored it. 'When you're finished, we'll talk.'

Megan pushed back the tray with a shaking hand, but he reached out and put his big warm hand over hers and said very softly: 'You're going to finish it all if I have to ram it down your throat.'

'Stop treating me like a child!' she said crossly.

'Then stop acting like one.'

She stiffened her shoulders and lifted her chin.

'And just shut up, Megan,' he said harshly. 'Every time you stiffen up like that, it means an argument.' He stood up, dragging his hands through his hair before linking them roughly at the back of his neck. 'I'm not in the mood for it.'

'What are you in the mood for?' she blundered.

'Oh God, don't tempt me!' His fists clenched at his sides and his face filled with dark red blood. 'Do you enjoy baiting me?'

'I'm s-s-sorry,' she stammered, stumbling to her feet. 'I didn't think. I—I——'

Richard stood there, shaking with anger. His right hand came up to rake through his unruly black hair, but Megan only saw it out of the corner of her eye and flinched violently.

'Good God! I wasn't going to hit you!' His shoulders sagged and he pressed his hand against his eyes. 'We can't even carry on a conversation without tearing at each other's throats.' He shook his head and turned away from her stricken face. 'I'll call Jim. He'll come and get you and take you some-where—anywhere. I don't give a damn any more.'

'No!' She ran after him as he reached for the doorknob. 'Don't send me away!'

'You can't stay here. A woman like you doesn't belong.'

'Don't say that! Please, Richard.' Dear God, she was begging him. Where was her pride?

Richard looked down at her hand digging into the bunching muscles of his arm and gripped it in his strong fingers. 'And what will you do if I let you stay?' His voice changed suddenly. 'Will you dispense your brand of "love" and make me happy?' he jeered softly in a hateful silky tone that made her flesh creep. Cold blue fires blazed in his eyes and his handsome features were twisted in a decided sneer.

She tried to pull away from him, but her

strength was no match for his. 'Let me go!'

'A minute ago you were begging me to stay. Isn't that just like a woman? Always changing her mind?'

She stopped struggling, trying to challenge him by her very calmness, until his grip loosened just enough for her to snatch her hand away.

'Well, Megan? What's it going to be? Shall I have Jim come and get you?'

Where could I go? she argued with herself as she looked into his face, noting strange lines of pain around his mouth and across his forehead that hadn't been there before. His eyes were bleak. She had to stay here. What if someone tried to contact her about her paintings? she reasoned. But she knew that wasn't why she wanted to stay. The thought of never seeing Richard again, never to hear that deep vibrant voice, never to see those striking blue eyes made her panic, but how could she admit to that? Oh, what was the matter with her? How could she dare entertain such a thought? He was married and she was playing with fire.

'I want to stay, Richard,' she heard herself say. 'But on my terms, not yours.'

His eyebrows rose. 'And they are?'

'I want to be of some use.' A burning warmth rushed to her face, but she kept her chin up. 'Outside the bedroom.'

'You can't go near Susan again,' he said, his eyes straying to the reddened gash on her cheek with the dark sutures still in it. 'And Charley doesn't need a babysitter. Do you expect to be paid to just sit around looking pretty?'

She returned his relentless stare until he had the grace to look away. One long white finger ran

through the thick dust on the chest of drawers
near the door. 'It seems to me you could use a
housekeeper.'

He stood looking down at her as if some fierce
inward struggle was going on in his head. His
breath became harsh and uneven, but he didn't say
anything.

She watched a slow colour creep up under his
tan. So much more was going on here than she
could understand. Unwilling compassion stirred in
her as she looked into his face. Tiny lines fanned
out from the corners of his eyes and she noticed a
glint of silver in the thick black hair at his temples
that wasn't there before. But it was the look in his
eyes that caught and held her. He looked wounded
and inexplicably vulnerable, and she wondered
what it was that had hurt him so deeply. Or was it
a person? Susan? Christina? His father? Surely not
herself?

'I don't require a salary,' she said softly, willing
to let him keep his pride. Every last dime he had
probably went towards Susan's medical bills.
'Room and board will be enough.'

'This house is a mess,' he agreed, blinking and
shaking his head as if coming back from a far
distant place. 'But it never mattered before. Ever
since Chris——' Bitter pain flashed in his eyes.
'Have you any idea how much work will be
involved?'

'I'm not allergic to hard work, if that's what
you're asking.'

'This house suffers from abuse and neglect,' he
pointed out. 'Do you honestly think a scrubbing
brush can erase it?'

'No.' Her calmness became an accusation. 'Your
house has to become a home to do that.'

His whole body clenched as if she had struck him, then he straightened his shoulders and turned away with a touch of arrogance before opening the door. 'All right, stay if you must,' he said curtly. 'I'll give you the room and board you asked for— but I won't believe you don't want any money. Your kind of woman always has a price!'

CHAPTER SEVEN

By the following afternoon, Megan felt the hollowness of victory. She was staying here on her own terms, but after spending the whole morning on her hands and knees in the living room, she couldn't see that she had accomplished anything. The surface dirt was gone, but the dust and grime were ground into the wooden floor and no matter how much she scrubbed, it didn't look clean. She had a feeling it never would.

'I think you've been at this long enough,' Franz commented, coming in from the kitchen. 'Whenever Christina scrubbed this floor, she said it was a losing battle—and she was a whiz at housework. Besides, lunch is almost ready and if you keep this up, you'll be too tired to eat.'

'Just let me get as far as the closet and then I'll stop.' Megan stretched stiffly, still on her knees, her hand rubbing the small of her back.

'Closet?'

'Isn't that what that door is?' She pointed to a small door in the wall opposite the fireplace. In the convent, it had been her job to clean the parlours and there was always a walk-in closet for visitors' coats.

'No, it's not a closet, it's Peter's study—Richard's now,' amended Franz.

'Oh,' she grimaced. 'One more room to clean!'

'I don't think he'll allow it.'

The scrubbing brush made a small splash in the bucket as she looked up. 'Why not?'

113

He rubbed the back of his neck and his mouth twisted as if he was debating with himself. He finally took a deep breath and let it out slowly. 'I'm not gossiping, mind you, but ever since the night his father died, Richard locked it, and as far as I know, no one's been in there since. It was Peter's favourite room before——' he let his voice trail off and shrugged almost apologetically.

'You mean he's keeping it as a—a shrine to his father?' Her eyes widened and she got to her feet, intrigued in spite of herself. 'Somehow I didn't think he was the type to do something like that.'

'I'm not,' Richard said coldly.

Both Megan and Franz jumped guiltily and turned to the hallway where he was standing, poised, just inside the door. His clothes were filthy and his face and neck were streaked with sweat and dirt from the fields. His eyes were a glacial blue and full of condemnation.

Embarrassed at being caught talking about him, she attacked. 'Why do you always have to creep up on us like that and eavesdrop on every conversation? It would have been polite to let us know you were there!'

'I was on my way to shower before lunch, Megan.' The formality of his tone was freezing. 'I heard Franz in here and I assumed—quite rightly—he'd be gossiping with you again.'

Megan gritted her teeth and stood rigid. He wanted to be formal, did he? She could be just as unfeeling. 'It wasn't gossip, Richard. I thought that door was a closet.' Her voice shook with such icy politeness it made Franz wince. 'Franz was merely correcting my mistake. He told me he didn't think you wanted me to clean in there.'

'He's right—I don't.'

She nodded stiffly. 'Very well.'

'And it's not because I keep it as a shrine. When I want privacy, it's a place where I can be totally alone. It's a soundproof room, that's all, so you can put your vivid imagination to rest.'

Her face flushed a dull red as she gathered up her bucket and mop and broom. 'Is there anywhere else off limits?' she asked through gritted teeth.

A maddening smile curved his mouth. 'It takes you a while, but you're learning, aren't you?' His smile deepened at her rising colour. 'You should have come and asked me that in the first place and saved yourself a lot of trouble.'

'Well, is there?' she snapped.

A laugh rumbled in his chest. 'No. The study's the only place I don't want you to touch. The rest of my father's house is yours—to clean to your heart's content.' With a flourish, he gave her a deep mocking bow and disappeared up the stairs.

'Some day,' Megan muttered under her breath, 'someone's going to take him down a peg or two. I only hope I'm around to see it happen!'

Franz grinned and took the bucket from her. 'That's what my mother says all the time. Even though she hasn't met you yet, she keeps saying you're the one who's going to do it.'

'Oh, I wish!' Just for a minute, she let herself relish the possibility and the satisfaction it would give her but then she knew it could never happen. 'Your mother's wrong,' she said defeatedly, following him to a small room at the back of the house where an iron washtub stood next to a washing machine. 'I'm no match for him. He gets the best of every conversation we have—and he knows it too.'

'Conversation? Is that what you call them?' he teased.

Her sense of humour surfaced and she had to smile. 'No, I guess that's too tame a word. "Altercation" is much better, don't you think?'

Franz laughed, and all through lunch they shared the private joke. Richard kept looking from one to the other, but they kept their faces innocently blank, and for the first time since coming to this house, Megan actually enjoyed herself.

Once the dishes were done, it was too hot to continue the housework, so she slipped her sketchpad under her arm and made her way outdoor, careful to keep away from Susan's windows. Jim told her he was keeping her heavily sedated now, but just to be on the safe side, Megan stayed on the opposite side of the house.

It was too beautiful a day to contact one of the art galleries on her list and have them give her the depressing news that they still hadn't located her paintings, so she resolutely put it out of her mind. A hot wind whispered through the tall weeds as her eyes swept the panorama of sloping, vine-strewn valleys, their precise rows heavy with burgeoning green and purple clusters under the cloudless sky. Richard specialised in growing Riesling grapes which Franz told her produced a rich spicy white wine, and the Shiraz, a black grape needed to make the more robust, amethyst-red wines.

Her fingers itched to get it all down on paper, to capture the living, breathing elements all around her. A deep drugging breath filled her lungs. Somehow the immensity of it all held a strange fascination for her and she found it hard to believe that when people talked of Australia, all they ever mentioned were the vast, shadeless plains of Nullarbor, the wild kangaroos and koalas, the aborigines, the terrifyingly beautiful Outback. They were here, to be sure, and worth mentioning, but there was so much more. The lengthening shadows deepened and reached out to her, touched something inside her and filled all the empty places in her heart. She belonged here.

A subtle change began to show in her sketches. As her long bold strokes became lighter shorter lines, the piece of charcoal almost had a will of its own. It flew across the paper balanced on her knees. Always before, her paintings held a wistful, haunting loneliness in them. But today, as she leaned back against the apple tree in the back yard, she was able to capture the beauty and grandeur and the latent power of the misty green valley. Looking at it, she knew she would never again be lonely. She would always remember this day and the deep feeling of contentment it brought.

From the landscape, she found herself sketching the occupants of the Talbot house. Starting with a shyly smiling Franz and then Susan, not as she looked now but as she used to when she was an actress, she went on to Charlotte. Letting her fingers take over without conscious direction, a piquant face looked back at her with large laughing eyes. She could look like that, she thought, if she wasn't afraid of being a girl.

That brought her to Richard. His was the easiest face to sketch, yet in some indefinable way, the most difficult. All the handsomeness was there under the unruly thick black hair, but his startling eyes kept looking at her, mocking her attempts to capture his rugged individuality on paper.

For a while she just sat looking at the sketch. Then, very precisely, she set it down on the grass beside her. All her movements were deliberate. She drew her knees up to her chin and clasped her hands around the paint-stained legs of her jeans, curling into a small tight ball, trying to shut out what she could no longer hide.

'Richard,' she whispered miserably, fighting against the devastating thoughts clamouring to be heard. Uppermost in her mind were three words that should never be said, three words that echoed faster and faster. She squeezed her eyes so tightly shut it made her dizzy.

I don't know anything about love, she argued with herself. I can't love him—I mustn't. But still the words were there, aching to be said. She opened her eyes and looked at the sketch and silently mouthed the words. 'I love you!'

But the painful admission didn't make her feel any better. 'I'm such a fool,' she whispered wretchedly.

A faint rustling of branches overhead penetrated her strangling thoughts and a sudden thump on Richard's picture startled her. A rag doll had fallen from the tree.

When she looked up, she stared into Charlotte's red face. Shock held her rigid for a second before she found her voice. 'What are you doing up there?'

There was a violent shaking of branches before the little girl swung herself out of the tree and landed on her bare feet on the dry grass. 'I was here first!'

'If you'd let me know, I'd have gone somewhere else and not disturbed you,' Megan told her.

Her expression was mutinous. 'I thought you were looking for me. I didn't know you were going to sit and draw pictures.'

'Why did you stay hidden when you realised I hadn't come looking for you?'

Charlotte ignored the question and tried to snatch the rag doll from the ground, but Megan was closer to it. She held it firmly, turning it over and over in her hands before looking up at her.

'Give it back,' she ordered stiffly.

Without a word, Megan handed the doll to her, expecting her to grab it and run. When she didn't, Megan gave her a tentative smile. Maybe this was her chance to try to heal the rift between them. 'Have you had her long?' she asked with just the right amount of unconcern.

Charlotte jammed the doll in her back pocket. 'My dad gave her to me when I was four.'

'I see.' Megan picked up her sketchbook and started to get up, but Charlotte shifted from one foot to the other in front of her as if she wanted to say something else. Megan relaxed back against the tree and waited. She had all the time in the world.

'Don't tell my dad I still have her,' Charlotte burst out. 'Dolls are for girls.'

'But you are a girl.'

'I should have been a boy.'

'Boys are all right,' said Megan reasonably, crushing back the pity that crept into her voice when she spotted a strong suspicion of tears in Charlotte's eyes. 'But if there were no girls, there'd be no more babies in the world. Can you imagine that? A world without babies?'

A tiny choking sob escaped Charlotte before she jammed her fist in her mouth. 'My dad said I never should have been born!'

Megan suddenly found it difficult to breathe. 'He told you that?'

'He was talking to Franz, but I heard him.'

'Maybe you misunderstood? There's an old saying about eavesdroppers never hearing good about themselves . . .'

'I didn't misunderstand. He told Franz my mother lost a baby boy in a car accident and he'd never . . . never forgive her for it.' Her little hands roughly scrubbed at her tears. 'Franz said he should be thankful he still had me. But he said I never should have been born!'

'Oh Charlotte!' Megan's heart stuck in her throat. Getting to her knees, she looked the little girl straight in the eye but couldn't find a thing to say. Dim echoes of Susan's rantings throbbed in her memory. '. . . he wanted a son instead of a daughter . . . it was an obsession with him . . . he calls her Charley instead of Charlotte . . . he's going to realise how wrong he is to stay away and come in here and see me and let me forgive him . . .' And Jim had said: '. . . he was punishing her . . . he wanted her to suffer . . . that's why he never would see her, why he kept himself so tantalisingly out of reach . . .' Now she understood so much.

She shuddered and opened her arms wide and without hesitating, Charlotte walked into them.

For long silent minutes she held the stiff, cold little body. Megan could sympathise with her. Even now, after all these years, she couldn't understand why her mother had abandoned her on the convent steps. She must have felt Megan never should have been born as well.

Finally Charlotte's shudders lessened and she drew away, wiping her nose with the back of her hand.

'Will you help me carry my things back to the house?' asked Megan gently, picking up her box of charcoal and sketch pad. 'It's getting late and you must be hungry. 'You've missed an awful lot of meals these past few days.'

Charlotte took the pad from her and buried her chin in her chest. 'I've been eating at Mrs Schmidt's house.'

'Oh. I wondered how you survived.' There was no reproof in Megan's tone, only a gentle understanding. 'Franz said something about spaghetti tonight. Do you like it?'

'Oh boy!' Charlotte's eyes sparkled and she grinned. 'He used to put beer in his sauce, but Daddy made him stop. Now he makes it taste Italian instead of German.'

'Hurry up and wash your hands, ladies.' Franz's eyes danced when he saw the two of them coming up the dirt path to the back door. 'My German spaghetti won't wait for ever.'

'Don't tell me you're putting beer in it again?' teased Megan.

He looked at Charlotte with mock anger, but his lips twitched as he waved them into the kitchen.

'I told her how you used to make spaghetti until Daddy showed you how to do it right,' Charlotte told him.

'Charley, you're letting out the family secrets,' he laughed.

'But Megan is family.'

His smile was wiped right off his face. He caught Megan's startled look and his eyes narrowed to blue fire before he nodded. 'You're right, little one—she is.'

And everybody seemed to accept her as such except Richard. He sat across the table from her at each meal, glowering coldly. If he noticed the closeness again developing between Franz and Charlotte and herself, he didn't acknowledge it.

But Jim Crawford noticed a change in her. When he removed the stitches from her cheek, he mentioned how well she looked and how pleased he was to see she was gaining back the weight she had lost.

'Just watch that you don't start getting fat,' he joked.

'Franz is such a good cook, it's a wonder I don't weigh five hundred pounds!' She gave him an impish grin and put her arm across Charlotte's shoulders. 'In between house-cleaning, Charlotte and I are trading recipes with him. Maybe I should see you about a reduction diet?'

He threw his hands up, horrified. 'Not yet, not yet!'

Richard was the only one who didn't laugh. He sat at the kitchen table watching them, yet he was strangely remote and set apart somehow.

Nearly a month passed and Megan flourished. The house began to lose its air of neglect and it almost became a home again. Almost.

Her days were slow and placid. It was only the nights that disturbed her. Many evenings she found herself lying awake far into the night, unconsciously listening for Richard. More often than not, he didn't come in, and she had no idea where he spent his time.

When he was there, he rarely spoke to her, but she was aware of his every movement, furtively

studying him when he was engrossed in his own
brooding thoughts. Her eyes would follow him
when he left the room and she often stopped her
house-cleaning to watch him through the shining
windows when he bent over his vines, checking the
ripening grapes.

The sun was high in a melting sky when she
found herself alone in the house one hot afternoon
towards the end of summer. She could have gone
swimming with Charlotte in the small lake not far
from the house, but she had one more bedroom to
clean and she wanted to finish it today. Richard
had disappeared for the past three days and since
it was his bedroom, this was the perfect time to do
it.

She nervously smoothed her hands down the
sides of her decrepit jeans as she walked along the
upper hallway, then mocked herself for the action.
There was nothing to be nervous about. Nothing
had really happened in this room. Everything was
shadowy and the heat was stifling even though the
days were beginning to shorten into autumn.
Megan steeled herself to ignore the memories of
the last time she had been in here; that would only
lead to something she couldn't face.

The window was stuck, but after a few grunting
pushes, it gave way, letting in a sudden rush of hot
air. She closed her eyes to let the heat-caused
dizziness pass before forcing her attention to the
work that needed to be done.

Thick dust was everywhere, but nothing was out
of place. From the looks of it, this could have been
an unoccupied room. But she knew he slept here
sometimes. She resolutely kept her eyes away from
the bed. 'I won't picture him here,' she said firmly,
clenching her fists and swallowing hard. 'I came

here to clean, not moon over some man.' After that, she felt better.

The cobwebs came away first and then the walls were dusted with a cloth tied over a long-handled broom. Franz would have helped her move the heavy furniture, as he had in all the other rooms, but he was busy in the vineyards today, so Megan struggled with them herself.

The carpet was hopeless; no vacuum cleaner or rug shampooer could change that. Without a qualm, she rolled it up and dragged it across the floor. It was heavy, but after a struggle she managed to heave it out of the open window. A self-satisfied smile spread across her sweating face as she waited for the dull thud to tell her it had hit the ground.

Instead, a loud grunt came floating up. She stood listening in the hushed afternoon stillness, but heard nothing more. Quickly leaning out of the window, she saw two long, jean-covered legs and boots sticking out from under the dirty, partly unrolled carpet.

'Are you all right?' she called down.

Silence was her only answer.

Panic sent her flying down the stairs and she was out of the door like a shot. Who would have been walking at the side of the house at this time of day? Jim never wore jeans, so she knew it wasn't him. Franz was in the vineyard somewhere and she would have heard the truck if he had come home. Was it one of the neighbouring vintners? Franz's brothers?

She grabbed one edge of the carpet and tried to pull it off the man. What if she'd killed him? Her hands were sweating and her hair slipped out of its knot, flying wildly about her white face as she jerked and pushed and pulled with all her might.

But it wouldn't budge.

She would have called for help, but there was no one to hear. She'd have to do this by herself.

'Oh, please be all right,' she muttered, struggling wildly.

She was on her knees in the thick weeds, breathing heavily, when she finally managed to move the carpet off him and she found herself staring into the one face she least expected to see.

'Richard!' Her hands flew to her mouth, her eyes wide with shock. 'Say something! Tell me you're all right!'

He was unconscious, his eyelashes lying like thick black fans on his cheeks.

With the hair on the back of her neck prickling, she hesitated only a moment before timidly slipping a shuddering hand into his shirt to feel for his heartbeat. A great surge of relief swept through her when she felt its solid drumming slowness. But she was too distraught to realize the significance of that. 'You're alive!' she breathed.

Her eyes quickly scanned her surroundings as if to will someone to come, but nobody was here to help. The only other person was Susan's new nurse who had come only this morning. Would the two of them be able to drag him into the house? But what if she did even more damage by moving him?

'Oh, Richard, what am I going to do?' she cried, biting her lip, fighting back her panic.

'You could try kissing me better,' he murmured.

Her whole body froze before she started to jerk away, but he easily reached out and gripped her wrist, keeping her hand crushed against his chest.

'Well?' he asked softly, his eyes blinking up at her, brightly blue and alert.

Megan could only gape at him. 'You're not very funny,' she accused breathlessly, trying to pull away from him. 'I thought you were hurt!'

His powerful arm closed around her waist, gently pulling her stiffly resisting body down on the ground beside him. 'I wasn't trying to be funny. I wanted to see if you cared.'

'Now you know.' She meant to say it sarcastically, but her hand on his thudding chest and the closeness of his face made her choking voice a husky, breathless whisper that sounded like a promise.

'What do I know, Megan?' He hesitated and gave her a long searching look before moving across her face to her scarred cheek. His hand reached out, smoothing her hair back from her face, gently tracing the angry red gash as if he would make it disappear.

Her mouth was dry and her breathing shallow. She was afraid to move and shatter the moment. She kept looking into his eyes, her own questioning and naked and vulnerable.

In slow motion his face came closer and closer. Then his eyes closed and his lips were warm and firm as they gently parted to rest on hers.

She had never thought to struggle against him or offer resistance of any kind. At the first touch of his lips, sanity fled. She was all glowing woman caught up in something totally foreign but irresistibly tempting to her innocence. Her whole body throbbed.

Compulsively, Richard's arms tightened around her, bringing her up against the entire length of him, clinging, stirring, sweeping her away on a sudden swift tide of surging passion. Like putty in his hands, her pliant body yielded, letting him mould her to his quivering length while his mouth blindly sought every singing nerve in hers.

His hands pulled her T-shirt out from the waistband of her jeans and roamed slowly up and down the shuddering length of her spine. When they spanned her ribcage and gently closed over the swelling firmness of her breasts, she could no longer reason. She could only feel and be tossed and blown and helplessly overwhelmed by a strange curling sensation that began in the pit of her stomach and tinglingly radiated to the rest of her.

His hands were warm, his calloused fingers gently feathering her heated skin with a langourous touch that was so beautiful and so right. The blood drummed noisily in her ears, suffocating in its tempo. When her own untutored hands answered his, timidly loosening his shirt and sliding and bumping uncertainly over the rippling muscles of his chest and back, she felt a shudder run through him and heard him harshly suck in his breath.

Without knowing how, she found herself on her back with her shoulders pinned to the gound. The tall weeds were all about them, rough and scratchy, but this sensation forced itself on her consciousness only an instant before it was replaced by another, more wondrous one: the unaccustomed solid, heavy weight of Richard's long body settling over hers.

She trembled with the burning desire he created in her, and for one breathless moment of suspended stillness, he looked straight into her face. She could see his eyes as big as saucers and as

bright and blue and fiery as the sky behind him.
The sun danced in the shimmering thickness of his
black hair and drew shadows in the deep slashing
grooves at the sides of his mouth. She kept looking
at him, totally submissive, listening to his ragged
breathing, feeling the uneven pulse hammering
against her fingers at the sides of his neck. Her
own heart raced madly in tune with his and she
couldn't drag her eyes away from him.

'Richard?'

'Don't say anything. Just let me love you,' he
murmured against her lips before mindlessly
claiming her mouth once again. Passion flared,
blasting into a bright consuming flame of desire
between them.

Blindly responsive, Megan could only follow
where he led. No other man had ever held her like
this, touched her like this, and the blood in her
veins sang a strange unfamiliar song that was
totally captivating. *Just let me love you*, echoed
with each wild beat of her heart. Her hands spread
across his back, digging into his damp skin. Her
heart soared and she arched mindlessly against
him with wanton abandon.

When he dragged his mouth away from hers,
burying it in the erratically pulsing curve of her
neck, she shuddered, moaning softly, 'Do you?'

He pushed himself up on his elbows, leaving his
hands to cup her face, his fingers twined in her
hair, his thumbs caressing her parted lips. 'Do I?'
he asked with a slight smile that slowly turned into
a vague frown.

'You said "just let me love you". Do you love
me?' Her face was full of radiant wonder.

She sensed rather than heard him catch his
breath as he looked down at her. Then she felt him

stiffen, his eyes turning a darker shade of blue and
losing the hard glaze of passion. It was slowly
replaced by an unmistakable twisting of pain
mingled with . . . contempt?

His whole weight crushed her for another
fleeting instant before she felt his defeated breath
harsh against her neck as he slumped against
her. Then he rolled away from her and got to
his feet.

A bewildering sense of shame began to curl in
the pit of her stomach as she peered up at him in
confusion. 'Richard?' And then suddenly she
remembered who she was and who he was.
Everything rushed back in a surging crimson tide.
Oh God! How could she? He was a married man!
Her legs were unsteady, but she managed to drag
herself upright and face him.

'Don't say anything—please!' she cried. 'I—I had
no right to even ask you such a thing.' An
hysterical sob rose in her throat and she stifled it
with a clenched hand across her mouth.

Mercifully, Richard didn't say anything. He
simply stood looking at her with an unreadable
expression, taking in her rigid figure and burning
face and wildly disordered hair.

Her body still throbbed from the demanding
pressure of his and she shuddered violently,
wishing she could erase the memory of such
wanton abandon. What was it about him that
could make a lifetime of rigid principles be
forgotten in his arms? Right and wrong had lost
all meaning in them. Hot colour surged into her
face and she prayed the ground would open up
and swallow her.

'Why the blush?' he asked bitterly. 'Your kind
doesn't do that.'

She caught a look of pain in his eyes and her throat closed. 'My kind. *My kind?*'

But what else did she expect? Hadn't she just behaved like a wanton? Richard didn't believe her innocence before; there was no way she could convince him of it now. Not after that mindless display. She closed her eyes in shame, but pride clenched her jaw and forced her chin up as she started past him.

His hand closed around her arm before she could take more than a step. 'You know I wanted you, Megan. I still do. But I can't tell you I love you. Is it so important to hear those senseless words? Does it make it easier? Do you make all your men say it before——'

'Let me go! Don't touch me!' She yanked her arm away.

'I'm not through with you——'

Huge green eyes glared up at him with icy fury before she shuddered into stillness. 'Oh-yes-you-are,' she gritted through her teeth. 'What about your wife? You might be able to forget her when it suits you, but I never will!'

Richard's head snapped back as if she had struck him. He could only stare at her, white-faced and grim. He drew himself up to his full height and, almost in a daze, he turned and let his long unhurried strides take him away from her.

Megan stood watching him until he was a tiny speck in the distance between the long rows of his vines. Then he blurred and dissolved as her tears slowly dripped down her face and on to her T-shirt and into her heart like burning acid.

CHAPTER EIGHT

MEGAN flung her brush down and blindly stared at the canvas on an easel near her bedroom window. For the past three days she had been like this, unable to concentrate on anything. Nothing was going right and she didn't know what to do about it.

She had been to Adelaide each day, doggedly tracking down an art collector who made yearly trips to New York. When she had finally got to see him this morning, he was polite but brusque, almost to the point of rudeness. He couldn't tell her anything about her paintings, though he knew the art gallery that sold them. When she left him, she had the vague feeling that he knew exactly where her paintings were, but he wasn't going to tell her.

She sighed in disgust at her paranoia and tried to focus on the canvas. It was a half-finished portrait of Charlotte. The girl's big blue eyes, intent and haunting, looked back at her. Only the eyes were complete; the rest of the small face was still only sketched in. But the eyes were vivid and alive and slightly condemning.

Jim knocked softly on her open door. 'Things not going well?'

'Oh, hello, Jim. They're not going at all, but I don't know what's wrong.'

He came to stand beside her and silently studied what she had done, then looked at her with half a smile. 'Those aren't Charlotte's eyes,' he said softly.

Megan stiffened, staring at the painting, her heart racing.

Jim shrugged. 'Or maybe the eyes are right, it's the rest of the face that's wrong?'

She mangled her bottom lip with her teeth. Why hadn't she seen it? She started to take the canvas and fling it aside, but Jim stopped her. 'Don't do anything you might regret.'

'I already have,' she choked, flinching away from those mocking eyes.

'It's not the end of the world. A lot of women fall in love with the wrong man. It happens every day.'

Her gasp was barely audible.

'I'm not blind,' he said gently. 'I suppose it was inevitable. He reacted so violently to you from the first. Usually it made no difference who came to care for Susan. But you, your innocence probably—he had to be attracted by that.'

Megan almost laughed at him.

He put his hands on her shoulders and gently turned her to face him. 'He's a good man, but not for you, I think. There's too much bitterness in him. I've got to get you away from here.'

Her sigh was utterly defeated. 'I know I should leave. I should return to St Ann's if nowhere else. They wouldn't turn me out on the street. But running away never solved anything. Somehow the thing I'd try to leave behind would always be with me.' Her thoughts went immediately to Richard. She felt again the surge of wanton response to his lovemaking and coloured with shame. 'There's a part of me I never knew existed, and it's difficult to face what I am.'

His forehead puckered into a deep frown. 'You talk as if you've committed some great sin instead of merely falling in love with the wrong man. You're spending too much time on morbid introspection. What you need is a change of scenery.' He glanced at his watch and looked back at her. 'I've got to make a house call on Franz's mother—that's why I came up here looking for you. Would you like to come with me? She's asked a dozen times when she's going to meet you.'

'I've been wanting to meet her too,' said Megan, 'but something always came up at their winery. Just give me a minute to change.'

'You're fine as you are.' His gaze slid from her jeans to her blue polka-dot blouse to her loosely coiled red hair. 'Emmi never stands on formality.'

'If you're sure,' she shrugged. Her jeans were the most comfortable thing she owned, and she found if she tied her blouse beneath her breasts to leave her midriff bare, it was perfect for these unusually warm autumn days.

Driving to Franz's parents' home, Megan felt caught up in a dream as they glided down several miles of twisting roads through a great sea of vines beginning to be harvested. A delicate softness was in the air and she caught the scent of fragrant-smelling grapes before they came to the crest of a hill and saw the sprawling white house below them. Set in a magnificent sweep of lawn, it was full of character and dignity and muted classical elegance. Ornamental camellia trees and native gums overshadowed a brilliant profusion of flowerbeds as they came closer.

In her mind's eye, she couldn't help but compare the Talbot house to this one. And she knew that, with all its faults and its haphazard air of abandonment and neglect, she wouldn't trade one moment of her life there for all the sunny existence in this idyllic setting.

Emmi Schmidt stood on the wide front porch with its soaring columns and shining windows and glossy black shutters. One of the many Germans who peopled this region, she was a big woman, as round as she was tall, with snow-white hair braided into a crown at the top of her head. Her face was darkly tanned and weatherbeaten into a fine web of wrinkles. She wore a long flowing caftan of thin white cotton, and although she looked a regal figure, Megan found her a most down-to-earth woman. Her disconcerting directness was her only flaw.

She smiled easily, welcoming them. 'So I'm finally going to meet the slip of a girl who's turned Richard Talbot into a human being again,' she smiled, reaching out to shake Megan's hand before beaming at Jim and waving them to sit in the comfortable chairs on her shady porch. 'I always said someone would bring him to his knees some day!'

She reached for a little silver bell on the table beside her and immediately a plump little girl with a long blonde braid falling down her back came to her. 'Some refreshments for our guests, dear. And tell your mama to come—I have someone for her to meet.'

The girl beamed shyly and turned wide hazel eyes in Megan's direction. 'Charley's Megan!'

'That's right,' laughed Mrs Schmidt. 'This is my granddaughter Elisabeth.' She hugged the girl, sighing softly and running a hand over her hair. 'Go, Lizzie, get your mama.'

'She knew me right away!' Megan was shocked.

'You sound surprised, my dear. Charley's talked

of nothing else for months. Even Richard has commented on your beauty. Only the other night, he was talking to my Hans. Your name was mentioned several times and with the strangest look on his face.' Her laugh was deep and booming. 'I've seen that look before, usually on one of my sons' faces when he found the woman of his dreams.'

Warmth rushed to Megan's face, but she pretended a sudden interest in the floor at her feet and kept her eyes down.

'You're embarrassing her, Emmi,' Jim cut in.

'Oh no, no, no,' Emmi said rapidly, her hands fluttering in her ample lap, 'I don't mean to embarrass you. But the change in Charley is so wonderful—and Richard too. Before you came, there was such a sadness about them. Now Richard is beginning to look the way he did when he was first married. You've worked a miracle!'

'But I've done nothing.'

'You call love nothing? Richard's beginning to live again. I hear he's starting to take an interest in things outside his father's house for the first time in years—why, he even laughs now! You've brought love to that family, my dear. Don't call it nothing.'

Megan gave her a troubled look and turned to Jim for help.

'Now, now, Emmi, you've probably heard some gossip and somehow got it twisted,' he told her.

'Gossip?' She looked offended. 'Franz tells me Richard's talking about buying into the winery. Is that gossip?' Her grey eyes flashed and she looked Megan up and down before narrowing on the thin red streaks on her cheek. 'He's like a dead man who's been raised to life.'

Jim shifted in his chair. 'It doesn't do to go jumping to conclusions where Richard is concerned. It might have been just idle conversation.'

'We'll see,' she said with a knowing smile, refusing to argue.

A tall fair girl in her middle twenties came out then, carrying a tray of glasses and a bottle of chilled white wine.

'Ah, Irmgard, come and meet our guest.' Emmi waved imperiously. 'Megan Crane, this is my daughter, Irmgard Stoessel.'

The girl dipped her head and smiled. 'How do you do?' she said shyly.

Megan liked her at once. 'Hello, Irmgard. Franz has told me a lot about you. I'm glad to have this chance to meet his favourite sister.'

'Franz speaks very highly of you too,' she said, looking through the fringe of her thick lashes. 'He thinks you're heaven on earth.'

Emmi chuckled, pouring the wine into stemmed glasses. 'Franz is my romantic. He used to balk at working in that house for Richard, but now he's up and gone before I am.'

'We know it's not because of Richard either,' Irmgard laughed. 'He didn't exaggerate when he said she was beautiful, did he, Mama?'

Emmi grinned at Megan's heightened colour. 'Very beautiful,' she agreed. 'And it's not just on the surface like so many these days. When you've finished your wine, would you like Irmgard to show you our house?' She spoke soothingly, but her eyes sparkled. 'My husband and sons built it, and now my daughters care for it like a work of art. I understand you're an artist and have an eye for beauty.'

'I'd love to.' She glanced at Jim. 'If it's all right?'

He nodded. 'We've got the time. I want to listen to Emmi's heart and check her blood pressure anyway.'

Irmgard welcomed Megan's interest, and once out of her mother's vicinity, overcame her shyness and began to chatter with enthusiasm. 'I'm so glad you came, Megan,' she smiled, showing her through the formal living room and dining room with its tasteful elegance.

Ivory texturised walls were hung with exquisite paintings done by local artists. Megan recognised some of their names as people she had met in her search. Their feet sank into Oriental rugs scattered on the dark floor and exotic tubs of flowers and ferns were everywhere. The furniture was a mixture of functional and comfortable, low sofas and straight chairs covered with a light washable fabric. The rooms were exceptionally large and had an open uncluttered look.

'This is a second home for all of us,' said Irmgard, 'so everything's washable and placed so there's space for the children. If they run, we don't have to worry about them bumping into anything and getting hurt.'

'There's a lot of love here,' Megan murmured lightly, running her fingers over a highly polished curving banister leading to an upper level. 'It shows.'

They followed thick muted green carpeting up shallow steps, and Irmgard grinned. 'Franz said you were more perceptive than most. Others who've seen this house have commented only on its beauty. But you realise what it is that makes this house more than just beautiful rooms with furniture in them.'

'This house is a home,' Megan said huskily,

thinking of Richard's house and how different it was.

As if reading her mind, Irmgard smiled sadly. 'Richard's isn't.'

'No.'

'But it could be.'

A troubled sigh escaped Megan and she turned to look out a small window at the top of the stairs. 'I doubt it.'

His house had been thoroughly cleaned so it didn't look so derelict any more, but it still wasn't a home. It should be filled with love, she thought with an ache of longing, but not mine. I haven't the right. It needs Richard's love to make a change, his love for his wife and daughter.

'It never was a home when Peter and Christina were alive and Susan was well,' Irmgard frowned. 'But surely that should be changed now—since you're living with him?'

The way she said it made Megan stiffen. *'Living with him?'* She slowly turned to the other girl, searching her face. There wasn't any sign of condemnation in her eyes, just innocent friendliness. 'I clean his house and I have a room there too,' she said haltingly. 'But I don't "live" with him. Not the way I think you mean it.'

Irmgard's eyes widened. 'But it's what I've heard people saying. After all, living with a man is an acceptable thing in America, isn't it?'

Megan was staggered. 'Maybe for some Americans, but not me. Does Franz think this too? He sees me every day. He knows the situation.'

She shrugged. 'As my mother says, Franz is her romantic.'

'And your mother?'

'She has an open mind,' she laughed. 'With ten

children and thirty-seven grandchildren, nothing shocks her.'

Megan was shocked beyond words. Yet she shouldn't have been. After all, they were un-chaperoned and Richard was a handsome, tragic figure of a man with his bedridden wife and shy young daughter. What could be more natural than that she provide comfort—of any kind—for this lonely man? But actually hearing it said made her skin crawl.

'Where are you going?' called Irmgard when Megan blindly started down the stairs. 'I haven't finished showing you the house.'

'Maybe some other time,' she said stiltedly. 'I really have to be going.'

'Oh, Megan, I'm sorry if I said something wrong.'

'It's nothing you said.' Her lips barely moved and her hands were sweaty on the banister. 'I should have realised . . .'

Somehow she managed to find the front porch again. Stumbling into the sunshine, she thanked Mrs Schmidt for a pleasant afternoon, but Jim noticed her colourless face and the pinched look about her mouth and realised something was wrong.

'I'll drive you back,' he said, rising to his feet.

'*No!*' With an effort, Megan controlled herself. This was happening too fast. She had to get away, be by herself so she could think things out rationally and decide what to do. 'I'd really rather walk,' she told him. 'It's not that far if I take a short cut through the vineyards.'

'Nonsense! It's much too hot and you haven't got a hat.'

They were arguing softly and neither of them

heard the truck on the gravel driveway. The sudden slamming of doors made them both turn their heads.

'Richard!' cried Emmi. 'And you've brought Marianna!'

Instinctively, Megan shrank back in the shade and squeezed her eyes shut. Why did he have to come now? All her emotions were in a turmoil. She was a seething mass of nerves, and she felt all he had to do was take one look at her and see everything she was feeling written all over her face.

When she ventured to look up, Richard was stepping on to the porch in front of Emmi with his arm around a tall slender girl with corn-coloured hair and dark eyes fringed with the longest lashes she had ever seen. If he saw Megan standing there, he gave no sign of it. All his concentration was centred on the girl's flawlessly made up face and moist parted lips.

'I ran into this beauty in town, Emmi,' he said lightly, smiling his warmest, most charming smile.

This was a Richard Megan had never seen before. Tall and smiling and very much at ease, he was dressed in a dark business suit. His grey striped tie was loosened and his jacket was open. Neat black boots were shining on his feet and he held a dark Stetson in his hand.

'Marianna, my dear!' Emmi embraced her with enthusiasm, 'I didn't know you were back.'

'I wanted to surprise everybody. Auckland was all right, but I found I missed all my friends too much to stay away a moment longer. Richard saw me in town waiting for a taxi and offered me a lift.'

'Thank you, Richard,' beamed Emmi. 'Wait

until this evening when Franz finds out you've come back home!'

'He's not here?' Marianna looked crestfallen.

'No, my dear. Didn't he write and tell you? He works for Richard now and spends most of his time there. He's turned into quite a good cook after all.'

'He cooks for you?' The girl's dark eyes, nearly level with Richard's, flashed him a bewildered frown. 'I understood you to have a housekeeper now—a redhead. In fact, you and she seem to have generated quite a bit of gossip——'

Jim cleared his throat noisily and nudged Emmi sharply in the ribs.

'Oh!' Flustered, she shook herself and tried to cover the awkward moment. 'In my surprise, I forgot to make the introductions. Megan Crane and Doctor Jim Crawford, this is my godchild, Marianna Schuler.' She stepped back and watched Jim take her hand and force a smile and then turn to draw Megan forward.

'Call me Jim, Marianna,' he said a trifle harshly, 'and this is Megan, Richard's housekeeper.'

A faint pink crept into Marianna's face, but it was a pale comparison to Megan's furious colour. 'I'm sorry if I said anything out of line,' she began.

'You didn't,' Megan said huskily, clearing her dry throat. 'If I hadn't been so blind, I'd have realised before now . . .' She caught her breath on a small sob and turned away, blindly starting for the steps. 'I really must get back,' she said briefly, hoping she wouldn't fall down the stairs and make a complete fool of herself. 'It was nice meeting all of you.'

'Megan, wait!' Richard's deep voice sounded close, but she didn't stop. She reached the driveway before her arms were gripped from behind, halting her in mid-stride.

Just for an instant, she was held back against him, every clamouring nerve in her body shuddering against his hard heated length. 'Let me go,' she choked.

'Why? So you can go on letting your imagination run away with itself?' He gave her a small push in the direction of his truck. 'Get in, I'll take you home.'

'No.' Her voice was high and tight. 'I'll find my own way.' She wanted to be alone, anywhere away from here, so no one could see her humiliation.

'You're only making it worse. They're all watching us from the porch. Get in.' Richard held the door for her and waved to the others. When she hesitated, he none too gently pushed her into the seat.

They reversed out on to the dirt road and Megan hugged her door, staying as far away from him as possible.

'Aren't you afraid you'll fall out?' he jeered after a few minutes as they bumped over the dirt road, rounding a curve so the house was no longer in sight behind the trees.

She didn't answer him.

'You didn't really think we were so isolated out here that a girl like you could live in my house and not cause a lot of speculation, did you?' he muttered angrily.

The heat that burned her face was suffocating. It had never occurred to her. She was so blind and innocent and trusting and stupid! But it wasn't all her fault. When she turned and looked at him, her eyes were full of accusation. 'All this time you knew people were talking about me—about us!

But you never said anything. You could have told me!'

'Don't blame me,' he said harshly. 'Blame your precious Jim. If he hadn't made such a big production out of finding somewhere else for you to live, no one would have remembered you were still out here. But no, he had to go around asking anyone and everyone.'

'Does Jim know what people are saying?'

'He's not deaf.' He gave her a sidelong glance and his mouth hardened. 'I don't understand you. You're not running true to form at all.' Abruptly he pulled the truck to the side of the road and cut the engine, leaning towards her, his big hand gripping her chin to bring her flaming face close to his. 'Why should it bother you, anyway? People talk about women like you all the time.'

The blank look she gave him was genuine—and then she remembered. He thought no more of her than any of the people gossiping about her. To him, she was a loose woman, available to any man if the price was right. 'I'm not like that!' she cried hysterically.

'Oh, stop, Megan. It doesn't matter any more. I thought it did, but I don't care how many men you've had before me. Just let me be the last.'

Her breath strangled in her throat. 'You don't know what you're saying.'

'I know exactly what I'm saying, and I mean every word of it. You're a beautiful woman with the face of an angel and a body that won't quit. Women like you were made to warm a man's bed. You're a gift from the gods.'

The sunlight and heat and silence all around them became thick and oppressive. There was not the slightest breeze yet Megan shivered as if her

body was suddenly wrapped in ice. 'I've never—
ever—warmed any man's bed.'

His raking glance ran over her from head to toe,
then he looked deeply into her big green eyes and
saw huge tears well up in them. He didn't speak,
didn't move. Something changed in his face and
the sound of his uneven breathing seemed to fill
the cab of the truck.

'People think you've been warming mine,' he
said unsteadily. A tear splashed on his hand and
his strong fingers brushed it away, but more came
to take its place. 'Why the tears?' he murmured
wonderingly. 'Would it be such a terrible thing?'

Unwilling images of herself and Richard, naked
in each other's arms, brought a low moan
bubbling up past Megan's parted lips. Somewhere
deep inside her, she glimpsed a tantalising
forbidden pleasure. A sudden frenzied desperation
curled in the pit of her stomach and her breath
quickened. She could feel herself shiver. It
wouldn't be terrible at all. It's what I want, she
thought, hating herself. And that made it all the
more shameful. Miserable colour ran into her face.

'There you go again,' murmured Richard, gently
amused. 'It must be the red hair.' His hands slowly
reached up to remove the pins holding it in its
knot. 'Is the blush because you're seeing the way it
would be? I can see it too. You and I . . .' His eyes
began to glow like burning blue diamonds.

She tried to say his name, but her voice broke in
the middle of it. The instant he touched her, she
was powerless to resist. All her bones turned to
water.

His mouth sought hers, parting her lips, and she
was drawn against him. The fingers of one hand
tangled in her hair while the other rested on the

madly pounding pulse in her throat. With
deliberate caressing slowness, his fingers moved
languorously on her skin, to the smooth flesh of
her neck, to the curve of her shoulders, descending
to unbutton her blouse. He untied it and cupped
her breast, letting its softness spill into his big
warm hand.

Her whole body clenched when his thumb
delicately stroked the rosy hardened nipple. There
was no hurry in him, no clumsiness, only a long,
leisurely, intimate exploration of her body that
sent a wild thrill of convulsed longing sweeping
through her.

She heard a faint breathless moan come from
somewhere deep inside. This wasn't enough.
Richard was formally dressed in a dark suit and a
white shirt with pearlised buttons that felt as big as
saucers to her untutored fingers. She fumbled with
his tie and undid the knot, but the shirt was giving
her trouble and she resented it. She wanted to rip
it from his powerful body and press herself against
all his solid warm flesh, lose herself in him, be
swallowed up in the security of his strong
muscular arms. Her fingers instinctively curled and
dug into the clenching muscles of his chest.

She wanted to offer herself for his total
possession, nothing less. But it would have to be
something less. Richard had a wife; she could
never possess him in return. There could be no
commitment between them, no equal give and
take, no unselfish sharing of love. Hollow passion
was a miserable substitute that would leave the
taste of dead ashes in her mouth.

'You're mine, Megan,' he murmured gently, his
quivering voice thick and husky and almost
exultant as he lifted his mouth at last, pressing

featherlight kisses against the pounding pulse in her neck. 'You were made for me.'

He let her draw back a little so she could look him full in the face and see all his inexpressible hunger. Her breathing was as ragged as his. 'No!'

He stopped dead, trying to smile—whether to reassure himself or her, she couldn't be sure. 'You don't mean that.'

'I'm not yours, Richard.' She choked back a sob, swallowing convulsively, her heart slashed to ribbons with every word of denial she uttered. 'I can never be yours.'

His face changed and his fingers tightened in her hair and held her head back. He looked straight into her eyes. 'Why?'

'You have to ask?'

'I don't understand, Megan. You can't deny you want me—every inch of your body is screaming it.'

She knew it was the truth; her yielding weakness made it obvious to both of them. 'Let me go. Please, let me go!'

He searched her flaming face for long dragging seconds before closing his eyes tightly. It was as if he was trying to shut out something that displeased him. His jaw clenched savagely. Then all at once he shuddered and pulled himself together and gave her a contemptuous smile, then he slowly released her. 'All right, Megan,' his voice shook. 'For now. It'll be better at home anyway. There'll be more room and no one to disturb us. It's not right that I take you here. A woman like you deserves——'

Megan didn't stop to listen to what he thought she deserved. She found the door handle and flung herself out on to the ground. Then she was on her feet and running as if the devil himself was after her.

CHAPTER NINE

THE next day was the worst in Megan's life. She packed and unpacked several times, torn between the need to leave and the insane desire to stay.

When she had come home last night, well after dark, Richard was nowhere around, Franz had gone home and Charlotte was already in bed alseep. She sat for a long time at her bedroom window, staring into an inky black sky sprinkled with glittering stars, searching for answers.

Where would she go if she left this house? Where could she go? How would she live? What would happen to Charlotte? The questions raced through her mind, making her head ache.

Nothing really mattered any more except that she leave here before she lost every ounce of self-respect she had. There was no question of whether or not she would lose it; it was only a matter of time until she did.

It was early when Charlotte knocked softly on her door expecting to see her still asleep. When she saw her open suitcase on the bed and the neatly folded clothes Megan was transferring to it, silent tears welled up in her eyes. 'Why?' she hiccuped. 'I thought you liked it here? I thought you liked me?'

'Oh, Charlotte!' Megan dropped the clothes and sat on the bed, drawing her close, folding her arms around her. 'You know I love you.'

'Then why are you leaving?'

'It's time for me to go.'

'You didn't come home last night,' Charlotte

mumbled into her shoulder. 'Daddy was worried and Franz said he wasn't surprised that you stayed away because Daddy's always so mean to you. Is that why? Because you're mad at him?'

'No, darling. It's just—oh, I can't even begin to explain,' she said helplessly.

'You said you'd stay. Franz said he thought you *loved* Daddy!'

Megan's breath caught sharply. 'He shouldn't have said such a thing.'

'Daddy's not really mean; Franz says he's just a lonely man. But everything changed when you came. He's not lonely any more. He even smiles at me sometimes, like he used to. You can't leave now. What'll we do without you?' Charlotte's little body burrowed deeper into Megan's shoulder and her arms tightened around her neck. 'You haven't even finished my picture yet,' she cried, as if that would make her stay.

'I'm so sorry.' Megan's voice was gentle and she wished there was some way to spare her. Why were innocent children always the ones to suffer from adult stupidity?

Suddenly the skin on the back of her neck prickled. She hadn't heard anyone come in, but she knew they were no longer alone. Looking up, she saw Richard standing in the doorway. Her eyes locked with his and the blood drummed noisily in her ears. Her hands started to sweat coldly as she held Charlotte in front of her.

'There's someone downstairs to see you,' he said, his voice cold and harsh.

She gaped at him before swallowing the sudden mad impulse to laugh. That was the last thing she expected him to say. After yesterday, she had imagined an altogether different confrontation.

Richard looked at the half packed suitcase on the bed and swivelled his gaze back to her. 'Let her go, Charley.'

Charlotte clung tighter.

'Stop your crying and act like a man!'

A jerking spasm shot through her and she straightened at once, scrubbing at her tears with the back of her hands.

Megan's jaw started to drop. 'She's your daughter, Richard, not your son!'

His expression didn't change, but his voice was curiously full of pain. 'If she's going to continue to live here with me, she'll have to act like a man. It's a hard lesson, but one she has to learn.' He flicked another look at her case. 'This is no place for weak or timid women.'

Megan got slowly to her feet, ice shuddering down her spine. 'Just what are you saying?'

'You're leaving, aren't you? That says it all.'

'You know why I'm leaving.'

He gave her a measured look, then let his eyes linger on her curving body in the simple sundress.

She stared back, steadily, refusing to lower her eyes.

'Charley, go tell the lady downstairs she'll be right there.' He spoke quietly, not taking his eyes off Megan.

Charlotte looked from one to the other. A strange seething tension was thick in the room and she didn't understand it.

'Now, Charley!'

Even after she had left, he continued to look at Megan. His hands were clenched into fists at his sides, his legs splayed wide as if bracing himself. But when he spoke, his voice was strangely unsteady. 'When you've finished packing, leave your case by the door. I'll take it down for you.'

'You don't have to.' Her chin lifted with faint pride. 'I may be short, but I'm not a weakling.'

His mouth twisted. 'Yes, you are, Megan. There are different kinds of strength—but I don't expect you to know what I'm talking about.' His quiet voice was full of regret. 'I think you missed out on your share of all of them.'

'Because I'm leaving?'

'Because you're letting gossip run you out. I thought you were different. I thought you'd stand up to it. You know you're not my mistress, so what does it matter what other people think?'

Her whole manner changed and her eyes flashed green fire. 'And Charlotte? She's just a little girl, Richard. What does she think?'

'I'll handle my daughter!' he cut her off harshly. 'You've got someone waiting downstairs to see you.' With a muttered oath he swung abruptly to the door and stalked out of the room, his back ramrod straight.

Megan mentally threw daggers into it all the way to the kitchen.

When she greeted Lora, his wintry eyes watched her, but she was determined not to let him upset her. In a little while she'd be gone and she'd never see him again.

'You didn't waste any time, Lora,' he couldn't resist taunting before turning to the sink for a glass of water.

Lora looked up in surprise. 'What do you mean?'

'Haven't you come to take Megan back with you?'

'Why, no.' She looked bewildered, turning to

Megan. 'Have you found a place? I know Jim's
been asking, but I thought he came up empty. If
you've found something, I'll be glad to take you.'

Megan shook her head. 'No, I haven't, but I've
got to leave anyway. You can understand that,
can't you?'

Lora jumped when Richard slammed out of the
back door, then her dark eyes gentled with
understanding. 'You've heard the gossip, then?
Jim said he thought you had.'

'Oh, Lora, I never dreamed ... None of it's
true!'

'I never thought it was.'

'You believe me?'

'Of course I believe you. Hey, this is me—Lora,
your friend.'

Megan's shoulders sagged. 'I thought ... Oh,
Lora!'

'You're forgetting I knew you before. You're
the last person in the world to be anybody's
mistress.'

Her face flamed and she buried it in her hands.
If she stayed it would just be a matter of time
before she was.

Lora put her arm across her shoulders and
smiled. 'Poor Megan! It seems we've been through
this before. Remember the ad you put in the
paper? You thought it was the end of the world for
you then, too, because people took it the wrong
way.'

A slightly louder choking sob was her only
comment.

'Cheer up, Megan. You're strong enough to
weather this storm, aren't you?'

'Strong enough?' She lifted her tear-stained face.
'Richard said I wasn't.'

'That's because he doesn't know you. If he did, he wouldn't say that.'

All at once an icy calmness settled over Megan. Her shoulders straightened and her chin lifted. How could she have forgotten all those years of gentle discipline behind her? The nuns had taught her to channel her emotions, put all her effort into thinking a thing out and deciding the right thing to do, then doing it without worrying what people thought. And here she was, letting her heart rule her head instead of the other way around. It was sheer folly.

'You're right,' she said softly. 'I was taught that it's better to see yourself truly than to care how others see you.'

Lora smiled and gently squeezed her shoulder.

Megan had to smile back in spite of herself. 'You're so good for me, Lora. What would I ever do without you?'

'I'm glad I was here,' said Lora. 'You know you can count on me—even after Jerry and I are married.'

'Oh, that's right, I almost forgot. How is he?'

'I thought so,' Lora said with mock anger. 'Jerry's fine. That's really why I came. I sent our wedding invitations to coincide with the end of the grape harvest, but there was a mix-up at the post office and a lot of people haven't got them yet. You promised you'd come.'

'Just name the time and place and I'll be there—with bells on!' laughed Megan.

'Jim said his house is big enough to accommodate us all. Next Saturday at six. All right?'

Megan nodded. 'I'll be looking forward to it.'

'I've got a million things to do before then.' Lora picked up her handbag and hugged Megan before turning to the door.

'If there's anything I can do to help . . .'

'I'll be sure to ask.' Lora's face was radiant as she waved goodbye.

With a wistful sigh, Megan watched her drive away before her attention was caught by Richard coming from the back of the house.

He watched the Volkswagen stir up a cloud of dust in the road before turning to her. 'You're not leaving?'

She thrust her head back to look steadily into his burning blue eyes. Despite the heat rushing up her neck, her voice was cool. 'May I stay?'

'The gossip will continue if you do.'

'As long as there's no truth to it, I won't let it bother me.'

'Is that a subtle warning, Megan?' He quirked a dark eyebrow in challenge.

She quirked her own boldly. 'Take it any way you like.'

His gaze ran over her upturned face flushed with fiery pride before he tipped his head back and laughed richly. 'I wasn't wrong about you, then. I'm so glad I wasn't wrong!'

On Saturday morning, Megan woke to a dim yellowish sunrise. Opening her window wide, she was surprised at the hushed stillness all around her. Usually her ears were assaulted each morning by heavy machinery competing with the laughing sound of pickers in the vineyards harvesting the fruit. But this morning there was nothing but an eerie waiting silence.

Franz was in the kitchen looking out the window when she came down. Noticing her worried look, he smiled in reassurance. 'See that thick bank of clouds to the west? It's going to storm today. We're lucky it waited this long. All the grapes are in.'

The sight of the boiling grey mass held Megan spellbound. 'Do you think it'll be a bad one?' She shivered, swallowing back an old, unreasoning fear.

'Probably not. Don't look so worried.'

She shivered again and sat down at the table in the yellowish dusklike darkness, gripping her hands together.

Franz tucked a rolled-up rain slicker under his arm and smiled warmly. 'I've got to meet Richard at the winery—but don't worry, I'll be back in time to take you to Lora's wedding tonight.' He touched a finger to his hat brim and disappeared outside.

The muted sound of thunder reached her, but she closed her ears to it, thankful that she'd be keeping busy with Franz's chores all day. I'll be so occupied I won't have time to think about rainstorms, she told herself grimly.

By early evening the storm hadn't broken, although she could still hear the ominous thunder rumbling in the distance. All day she watched the sky with its boiling clouds and hissing wind and fought against a nameless fear that was worse than any storm. She hated rain and always associated it with the day she had been abandoned on the convent steps. It was raining then and her mother had rung the bell before rushing away, telling her to go with the nuns when they answered. 'I'll be back for you,' she said. But she never came back, and Megan never knew why. No one had ever heard from her again.

Her fingernails dug into her palms as she stood at the kitchen window waiting for Franz. It was five o'clock in the afternoon, yet the sky was as black as midnight. Charlotte was engrossed in a television programme and Megan wished she could be that oblivious to the weather.

She smoothed her hair in its braided coil at the back of her neck and resisted the impulse to run her hands nervously down the sides of her dress. Made of emerald green silk, it fell from one shoulder to her ankles, toga-style, its brilliant colour intensifying her deep green eyes. She wore the gold rose necklace Lora had given her and on her feet were narrow, gold spaghetti-strap sandals.

At the sound of tyres crunching on gravel, she reached for her evening bag, and forced a smile when Franz gave her a long low whistle of appreciation.

'Beautiful and punctual,' he grinned. 'I'm a lucky man tonight. Is Charley ready? Lizzie's been waiting all afternoon for this slumber party my mother cooked up.'

'Here I am!' Charlotte bounced into the kitchen with a duffel bag in her hand and smiled at the darkness beyond the windows. 'We're going to tell ghost stories tonight. Isn't the weather perfect for it?'

Franz laughed and held the door open for them. 'Just don't go scaring Lizzie half to death.'

She giggled, slipping her hand into Megan's. 'I've already promised Megan not to.'

The air was hot and still and heavy when they dropped Charlotte off and drove through the dark countryside to Jim's low, sprawling ranch-style house. When they turned into the drive, he was waiting on the shallow porch steps looking harassed but grinning broadly in a trim black tuxedo.

'I'm acting father of the bride tonight, but I'm nervous as a cat,' he said jerkily, looking at the sky. 'I only hope the rain holds off for another ten minutes.'

Franz slapped him on the back with one hand while shaking his hand with the other. 'Spoken like a true father,' he joked. 'All your patients should see you now! You must be nervous if you haven't noticed how beautiful Megan looks.'

'Oh.' Jim swivelled his head in her direction, then smiled apologetically.

'He's just teasing you,' she smiled, coming to stand beside him. 'We'll talk later, after the ceremony.'

Folding chairs had been set up in the spacious living room and they found two empty places at the back just as the minister nodded to an elderly woman sitting at a grand piano in the corner. When she struck the first chords of the wedding march, an expectant hush fell over everyone and they all turned to see Lora.

Only Megan missed her entrance. Just as Lora came in, Jerry walked from a flower-decked side alcove followed by his best man, Richard Talbot.

Megan was so surprised she couldn't look away from him. Like Jerry, he was dressed in a formal black tuxedo. But unlike him, he stood easily, faintly bored. When he turned his eyes locked with hers as if he had known exactly where she was from the moment she came in.

A slight gasp stopped somewhere in the middle of her chest, cutting off her breathing. He might have been the only other person in the room, for everything receded but him. Her soul stood in her eyes and she couldn't turn away. His hair was thick and black and shining, his eyes a glittering bright blue. Broad dents slashed the sides of his face when he gave her a wry smile. She looked at the bold sensuous line of his lips and trembled, a strange warmth curling in her stomach as if they had touched her.

He turned away then, to hand Jerry the ring, but she kept her eyes riveted on him, seeing, hearing nothing else.

When Franz's supporting arm at her waist gently shook her, she turned blindly.

'Are you all right?' he whispered.

Her whole body shook, breaking the spell, and she realised the ceremony was over. She had missed it entirely. Swift colour rose to her face, but she smiled brightly, trying to hide her embarrassment. 'Weddings are emotional things, aren't they?' she managed to murmur.

Franz must not have noticed her breathless preoccupation, because he laughed gently and ushered her into a noisy laughing group of people circling Lora and Jerry, tossing rice and offering congratulations.

Lora's gown was understated elegance itself. Floor-length white satin inset with lace gave her angular figure a look of fragile delicacy. Her dark hair was swept back under a frothy veil of white net and her face was radiant. Tiny white flowers were in her hair and she carried a small bouquet of white roses nestled in gypsophila.

All evening her happiness tried to extend itself to Megan. She was for ever dragging someone away from an engrossing conversation to introduce him to her. Several doctors were there, and their wives, and many of the interns and nurses from the hospital. They would smile, but Megan noticed it didn't reach their eyes, and for a while she

wondered why. They would converse lightly with
her for a few minutes until Lora was called away,
then they would excuse themselves and leave her
standing alone.

At first she didn't realise what was happening.
Lora tossed her bouquet and left with Jerry in a
shower of rice and confetti—and then Megan
noticed a distinct change in the atmosphere.

It began subtly enough. Jim was occupied with
his duties as host, Franz was busy flirting with a
vivacious nurse, Richard was deep in conversation
with Jim's wife. Only Megan was a fish out of
water. She spotted Jim across the room and
started towards him. When she passed a circle of
brightly chattering women, a sudden unnatural
silence descended. She stood absolutely still,
unable to move, as a finger of ice slithered down
her spine. It had happened at other times during
the evening, but now it was becoming blatant.
Then, all at once, she knew.

The blood rose hotly to her skin. Beneath the
softly draped folds of her emerald gown, her knees
shook. She couldn't deny it or pass it off as being
over-sensitive. They were talking about her. They
must have noticed the way her eyes followed
Richard all evening. However unwittingly, she had
added fuel to the already burning gossip about the
two of them.

No matter how much she told herself it didn't
matter, she felt raw and vulnerable. Turning
blindly, she found the bar and recklessly reached
for a bottle, any bottle, and poured herself a drink.
She had had nothing stronger than fruit juice all
evening, but she felt the need for something
stronger now. Just as she raised the glass to her
lips, Richard's mocking face came into her line of

vision. He stood there, tall and still, silently daring her to go ahead. Blind stubborn pride gave her the strength to continue the motion without checking it, pretending she hadn't noticed him.

But once she took a long thirsty swallow—as she had seen people do in films and on television— she couldn't have been more shocked. It was as if she poured acid down her throat. Her eyes stung and her breath was choked off.

Richard was still watching her, ready to enjoy her reaction, no doubt. Rather than give him the satisfaction of seeing how stupid she was, she stiffened, raised her head almost regally, and managed to keep her face expressionless before turning blindly in the direction of the kitchen.

Fortunately, no one was there, and when the door closed behind her, she doubled over, letting out her breath on a strangled choking cough and gasping violently.

With her hands clutching her throat, she ran to the sink. Maybe water would put out the fire she had swallowed. It was cold, sliding down her throat, but she was sure it would take at least a gallon to help her breathe normally again.

A soft breathy whistle made her stiffen, but she was able to compose herself before she turned to face whoever had come in behind her.

CHAPTER TEN

'I TAKE back everything I said about you being weak,' Richard said softly, putting a hand under her chin and gently turning her face up to his. 'You never batted an eye when you swallowed that whisky. You're the first woman I've ever seen drink like a man and still remain feminine.'

Megan knew she should say something scathing, but she couldn't talk. She was sure her vocal chords had been burned and she would never speak again. She could only look at him with huge eyes.

'I know what you've been going through the last two hours,' he said gently. 'I stood back and watched and listened. It's so much worse for a woman than a man, isn't it?' His face softened and his eyes shone. 'You've been snubbed by everyone because of me. But you didn't let it throw you. You defied every one of them with your very silence.'

She still couldn't speak. Her bitterness turned to confusion and her breathing quickened. A warm disturbing sensation fluttered nervously in the pit of her stomach before uncoiling and radiating to the rest of her.

'You're the woman I've been looking for but never thought I'd find,' Richard said unsteadily, drawing her closer to him, burying his face in her neck helplessly.

Megan closed her eyes and shivered. All evening he had kept his distance; now he was here. Could she really be hearing this? Her arms came up to feel his solid broad back and warm muscles rippled through the cloth. He was real, not some figment of her imagination. Unthinkingly, her hands clenched as his lips softly fastened on the long warm curve of her neck, sending shudders pulsing through her body. Swallowing, she couldn't make any sense of it all.

'Say you're mine, Megan,' he murmured mindlessly against her skin, his hands restless. They slid down the quivering length of her spine before resting on her hips, inexorably drawing her closer.

Of course she was his. Was there ever any doubt?

But he was not hers. Susan's strident voice rang in her ears: *'I'll never let him go!'*

With a groan of anguish, Megan tried to twist out of his crushing embrace. Her struggles finally reached him, and when his hands fell to his sides, his eyes were glazed.

'Come with me,' he pleaded. 'Stay with me. Be my wife. Everything you were in the past is behind you now, and it'll stay there. You know your future's with me. It was there in your eyes when I first saw you tonight.'

Her breathing was ragged, but she stood stock still in front of him, both hands clenching the edge of the kitchen sink behind her for support. 'You know that's impossible.'

All at once a brilliant blinding flash of lightning ripped the stillness between them and she flinched so violently she nearly fell. She turned her back to him, not wanting him to see the stark fear that sprang to her eyes. She had fought it off all day, but now it was closing in on her. The thunder was deafening and she jammed a hand to her mouth to stifle a stricken cry.

'You're afraid of storms,' Richard laughed softly, wrapping his strong arms around her in protection, resting his chin on the top of her head. 'You don't have to be—I'm here. Let me take care of you. I promise nothing will ever hurt you again. How could I let it?'

She turned blindly to him, terrified by the quick broken flashes of lightning, and her cry was muffled against his chest. 'Yes. Yes! *Yes!*' Her fingers clenched convulsively in his shirt. 'Help me, Richard!' she cried, her whole body shaking.

He was all gentle loving concern in the face of her mounting fear. 'We'll go home now.'

He swiftly made their goodbyes, shielding her from the raised eyebrows and knowing looks of some of the guests. Jim's questioning glance was waved away. 'She's afraid of the storm,' he said in explanation. 'Tell Franz she's coming with me. If we leave now, we may beat it.'

But they didn't. Halfway home, the torrent burst and Richard had all he could do to keep his wind whipped truck on the road. Rain lashed at them. No matter how fast the wipers scraped the windshield, he couldn't see anything but a solid wall of water reflected in his headlights.

The temperature dropped sharply and a roaring wind rose, lashing the rain at them, grotesquely bending the topmost branches of trees nearly to the ground. Jagged streaks of lightning split the seething sky, only to be followed by the ear-shattering pounding of thunder.

Megan clenched her hands tightly together in her lap and tried to concentrate on the lighted dials of the dashboard—anything to block out the memories boiling inside her. But they spilled over and her head fell back against the seat and acid tears coursed down her face.

'No!' she cried, wringing her hands together, forgetting everything but the sound of the wind and the rain and the lightning and thunder. She couldn't remember her mother after all this time, but she remembered her fear at being left alone in the rain. 'Don't leave me! Please, don't leave me!' she moaned.

As they drove on, her face became ghostly white. A fine sweat stood out on her upper lip and her eyes were distended and filled with terror. She was far away from here, lost in her own private world of loss and rejection and abandonment. Why had her mother left her? Irrational guilt came welling up. What had she done that was so terrible—terrible enough to make her mother give her away? If only she could find out and undo it, even now, after all this time. If only . . . If only . . .

'Megan!' Richard tried to make himself heard over the loud drumming rain. 'Are you all right? We're home.'

She didn't hear him. She didn't feel his powerful arms gathering her rigid body close. She didn't see his look of concern.

When he slid out of the truck, cradling her in his arms, the torrential rain pounded on his shoulders and his feet nearly shot out from under him in the slippery mud, but he somehow managed to keep his balance. Megan's dark red hair broke from its braided coil and was plastered against his face and neck, blinding him.

The cold rain splashing in her face brought her to her senses and she was dazedly aware of a door slamming behind her and Richard carrying her, dripping, through the hushed and darkened rooms of his house.

Lightning flashed in blinding brilliance, then blackness once again surrounded them with eerie irregularity. Violent thunder assaulted her ears. Rain pounded and shook the windows and high winds howled past like screaming demons.

Richard stopped at the door of his study and gently set her on her swaying feet. When he turned his key in the lock, thunder shook the house. Megan shrank against him but he smiled and curved his arm around her, murmuring soothingly. 'Nothing will hurt you, Megan. You're mine. I'll never leave you.' He led her gently into the dark room.

It was quiet here. The rain seemed strangely distant. Even the savage thunder was a dim muted echo.

Richard didn't turn on a lamp. He shrugged out of his soaked jacket and damp shirt and sank into a low leather chair, pulling Megan on to his lap and holding her close.

Her gown was mud-splashed and dripping, but she was beyond caring. Like a child, she burrowed into his naked chest, seeking shelter in his powerful arms, breathing in the comforting musky scent of him, feeling warm and protected for the first time in her life. She was safe. She belonged to him. She had come home at last.

Neither of them knew how long they stayed like that, listening to the storm. Neither of them realised exactly when it stopped or when they drifted into sleep in each other's arms. Megan's face was pressed into Richard's neck, her arms entwined with his, her hair a vivid red fire tangled in his knotted hands.

Shortly before dawn, they stirred, each waking the other.

Her eyelids flickered open and she met his smouldering blue gaze. 'Richard?' she murmured.

He smiled almost in bemusement and tightened his arms, imprisoning her in the small warm circle. 'This is where you belong, darling. Every morning for the rest of our lives we'll wake up this way.'

Megan held her breath, wishing she didn't have to fight him any more. She wanted only to love him.

'Say yes,' he demanded raggedly, but he found her mouth with his before she could answer.

Her lips parted and she felt the hard strength of his mouth and the warm caressing power of his hands. Her whole body was alive and pulsing. 'I love you,' she breathed against his lips. 'I know it's wrong, but I won't deny it any more. I love you.' Arching her arms upward around his neck, she dug restless fingers in his hair and pulled him closer, uncaring that the thin silk of her gown slipped down and nothing was between them. The rounded thrust of her breasts flattened against his naked chest.

'This isn't wrong,' he muttered angrily, suddenly drawing back and cupping her face in his clenched hands, his eyes glittering dangerously. 'Don't you understand? It won't be just an affair. I want you, all of you—not just the loan of your body for a stolen hour. Marry me. Be my wife.'

Megan stiffened and held both hands flat against his chest to stare into his savagely demanding face. 'You know that's impossible!'

'Why? Won't you give up your freedom even for me?' He let his arms fall lifelessly to his sides. His lips twisted after a moment, his voice became too low, too quiet. 'Or are you after bigger game? Is that it? I'm not a wealthy man, but I can provide a decent life for us.'

She shuddered, sliding off his lap and hitching up her dress, hating herself but hating him more. 'I told you before, it isn't a question of money.' She struggled to keep her voice level. 'Maybe you don't have a conscience, but I do. I can't pretend you don't already have a wife. She's there, and nothing you can say can make her suddenly disappear.'

'Not any more.' He pushed himself to his feet to face her squarely. The grim line of his mouth thinned and his face became cold and hard. 'There's an old saying, "Let the dead bury the dead". I never knew what it meant until that afternoon you threw the carpet out of the window and hit me with it.'

Megan's eyes widened.

'Don't you remember throwing my wife at me then, too? You were so full of passion and promise, but then, somehow, you brought her between us. You said you couldn't forget her—but God help me, that was the first time since she died that I really had forgotten her. Always before, I let her memory twist everything I did. We're alive, you and I, she's dead. I've finally let her go after all this time. Her memory won't distort my life any more.'

She was totally confused. He was saying so much, but she couldn't understand. She dropped her eyes, trying to shift away from him, but his hard fingers dug into the bones of her face, making her look up at him.

'Don't you see? I thought I buried her three years ago,' he grated, 'but you made me face it. I went through her funeral, but I didn't really accept her death—until now.' He drew her closer, curving her resisting softness to the taut power of his body. 'She's gone, Megan. Don't bring her between us. I'm asking you to marry me.'

'I don't understand you!' she cried, struggling against him. 'All this talk about her being dead and buried. Susan told me she wouldn't let you divorce her. You can't pretend she's already dead!'

She felt his whole body stiffen convulsively and the steel grip of his fingers was crushing. Long shuddering seconds passed before his breath was finally expelled in a hiss. Then his arms fell away from her to hang at his sides and he took a rigid step away, his face white with shock, his eyes deeply blue and distended.

'Susan told you that?' he choked.

Megan turned away, pressing a hand to her mouth. 'She—realised I loved you even before I did. That's why——' Her fingers trembled over the angry scar on her cheek. 'She told me over and over you were hers. She'd never let you go.'

'Look at me.' Richard's voice was harsh. When she didn't, he roughly gripped her chin, forcing her to face him. 'She lied to you, Megan. She lied! She-is-not-my-wife!' He said each word coldly, precisely, in a hard unyielding voice. 'She has never been my wife!'

Megan stood absolutely still, but the floor kept rocking beneath her feet. All the colour left her face and all she could do was gape at him. 'I don't understand,' she faltered, a fine tremor running all through her. Then all of a sudden her eyes widened. 'Your *father's* wife?' she breathed, stunned.

He nodded grimly. 'Susan was his fatal mistake.

He thought marriage to so young a woman would
keep him young. He didn't realise she'd be the
death of him—and my wife—and my son!'

Megan felt all her strength leave her. She would
have fallen if he hadn't reached out and caught
her, gathering her close to his quivering length.

'I thought you knew,' he muttered. 'I've heard
you mention Christina. Someone must have told
you?'

She shook her head. 'Every time Franz tried to
tell me something about you, you told him to quit
gossiping. Susan was the only one—and she told
me you were hers. She'd never let you go.'

'God!' Pain was in his voice as it rumbled
against her. 'She's got a lot to answer for!'

'Will you tell me?' she whispered, trying to
understand, but still baffled.

Richard stood for a long time, searching her
face with pain in his eyes. 'I suppose I owe you
that much.' He held her away from him. 'My wife,
Christina, was pregnant with our second child
when I came home from college to help my father
with his vineyards. I told her she was beautiful,
even though she thought she was awkward and
heavy. But while I was working in the fields, Susan
was busy working on her. She convinced her that I
found her unattractive, that I didn't love her any
more, that I preferred my father's wife to her.

'I didn't realise what was happening for a long
time. I kept thinking it was her condition; she'd be
all right after the baby was born.' His lips twisted.
'But no matter what I said, she wouldn't believe
me. In the end, I stopped trying to reason with
her. I think I actually began to hate her then
because she wouldn't trust me. She had no faith in
me.' His expression was grim, his face haggard.

'Then my father began believing Susan's lies. Their marriage was breaking up, and he blamed me.'

The silence was endless. He didn't seem to breathe at all. Megan touched the harsh planes of his face and he shuddered, crushing her to him, his taut body straining against hers as if to absorb comfort from her.

'I wanted to leave, but my father needed me, so we stayed,' he muttered. 'The final blow came when Chris left me—and Charley. Susan talked her into it. She was even driving her to the airport to make sure she left when the accident happened. Somehow they skidded into a ditch. They were both trapped inside the car and by the time I got to them, Chris had lost a lot of blood. I tried to get her out, but she died in my arms—cursing me!' His face whitened as he relived it. 'Susan kept screaming for me to help her, that Chris was dead and I couldn't be of any use to her now. She kept screaming and screaming. I didn't try to help her, Megan.' He shuddered. 'I just sat there, holding my dead wife.'

He released her and stepped back, breathing short ragged breaths. His face was ashen and she could see sweat beading his anguished features.

'When they were finally rescued, there was no way they could save the baby Chris was carrying. It was a boy, they told me later. My son!' He ran his hands roughly over his face to scrub away the remembrance. 'She killed my wife and my son!'

Megan couldn't say anything. After a long time, Richard lifted his head and looked at her with bloodshot eyes.

'I blamed my father for marrying Susan in the first place. I accused him of all kinds of irrational things. I laid all my guilt on him and lashed out at him with all the cruelty in me. That same night, he died of a heart attack in this very room.'

She gasped, shivering.

'Not a very pretty story, is it?' he muttered. 'That was three years ago. I gave up living then. All I could do was hate—and keep Susan alive so I could continue to hate. That's why I kept her here and why I stayed and why the house was such a mess.'

'And you still hate,' said Megan numbly, knowing that even now he hated her—because she was a woman.

'Don't I have the right? My God, look at what she did!'

A thin shaft of anger mingled with the pity running through her. 'Maybe you do, Richard. What she did would have broken a lesser man. But you're strong enough to bend. Why did you have to transfer that hate to all women?'

'Not all women,' he said harshly. 'Not you.'

'Oh yes, me. Deep down, if you're honest with yourself, you'll admit you despise me because I'm a woman.' Megan sighed before looking straight into his eyes. 'You've never treated me with respect—we both know that. And what about your daughter? She's going to be a woman some day. Even though you're trying to turn her into a boy.'

There was a long tight silence before Richard turned away and reached for his hopelessly wrinkled shirt. He shrugged into it and buttoned it slowly before turning to her with sombre eyes. 'You're right about Charlotte,' he said heavily, at last. 'But not you. Somehow you're different.' He shook his head. 'I don't know what it is. Maybe it's because you've had so much experience with

men. There's never been any need to pretend
with you—you've always known exactly what I
am.'

A sudden rush of heat to her face made her turn
away.

'What's the matter? That was a compliment——'

'I don't know anything about men!' she cried,
jerking away from him when he would have
touched her.

But he went after her, fiery possession in his
eyes. Fastening his hands on her hips, he pulled
her towards him, grinding her body against his
taut thighs, making her aware of his arousal.
'You're mine, Megan. I don't hate you because
you're a woman. God help me, I love you!'

A long sweet shiver ran through her entire body
before she realised this was a gesture of intimacy
that should have appalled her innocence. But it
didn't. She belonged to Richard, whenever,
wherever, however he chose to make her his. No
wife stood in the way now, nothing—except her
innocence.

Her eyes flew up to his. 'There's only you,
Richard. There's never been anyone else. Can you
believe that? You must believe me.'

He opened his mouth to say something, but
before he could utter a word, her whole body
wrenched away from him and she was stunned
into stillness, her eyes glued to the wall behind
him. 'Where did you get those paintings?' She
shuddered violently and stepped closer, touching
the canvas with shaking fingers.

There were two paintings, one slightly larger
than the other. Both in expensive frames, both
were striking and full of a gripping loneliness. The
background was all seething, grey and purple fury,

and there, off to one side, stood a small boy with big grey eyes, his hands stretched out in silent supplication.

'I found them for you, Megan.' His voice was strangely quiet but full of emotion. 'John Hunter had them and sold them to me. I made him promise not to tell you where they were.'

John Hunter, the collector who made yearly trips to New York. Megan closed her eyes and all her breath left her.

Richard came to stand beside her and took her hand, linking his fingers with hers, looking at the portraits. 'Once you found them you'd have had no reason to stay. I couldn't let you go until I'd made you mine, so I made him promise.' When she didn't comment, he asked very quietly: 'What happened to the boy?'

'I don't know,' she faltered. 'He was adopted and I couldn't find out who—or where——'

He dropped her hand roughly and stiffened. *'You gave him up for adoption?'*

She dragged her eyes away from the paintings and stared up at the sudden white rage in his face, her mouth falling open in surprise.

'How could you?' he accused. 'Was it too much trouble to keep him? Did you convince yourself you were doing the noble thing?' His whole body shook with disgust. 'Where's your soul? You could paint him like that and then give him away!' He turned away so violently that she flinched.

She was stunned into silence, staring at his rigid back, the repudiating set of his shoulders, the uncompromising clenching of his hard angular jaw. 'No,' she choked in a softly dying whisper. At his sound of disgust, she became frighteningly calm. 'I didn't give him away, Richard. I wouldn't have been strong enough to do it.' The look of scorn he threw over his shoulder made her stiffen icily, squaring her shoulders and lifting her chin. 'It does take courage, you know. I would have kept him if I could have done, but he wasn't my son! You were wrong to jump to that conclusion.' Her stomach plunged. 'But it's so much easier for you to think the worst of me, isn't it? So much easier to condemn——' Her voice wobbled, betraying the fingerhold she had on her emotions.

Richard turned quickly, his face whitening. Taking her shoulders in a grip like iron, he said thickly, 'Megan, I——'

She twisted away savagely, freeing herself from his grasp, and rounded on him, shaking with fury. 'Don't you dare say anything! I don't want to hear it! Anything there might have been between us is finished!' She ground her teeth, knowing with terrible finality that it was true. 'The only reason you believed such a thing was that you wanted to believe it.' Her voice broke then and she turned, keeping her quivering chin high, refusing to let him see the huge tears standing in her eyes.

But it was only a heart-stopping moment before he came up behind her, his hands clamping on the soft flesh of her upper arms to hold her still when she would have pulled away from him. The heat from his body burned her back and she struggled, trying to twist away from him. Instead, she was turned in his arms and crushed against his shaking length.

'I'm not letting you go. You're mine!' he demanded before his mouth ground against hers.

There was a violent explosion of her senses as she struggled for breath, and then voices impinged on her consciousness. A deep booming thundered in her ears when Richard lifted his face away from hers, stiffening in a listening attitude.

Someone was pounding on the door before it burst open and Franz and Charlotte stumbled in.

'Daddy! Daddy—we've been looking all over for you. Doctor Crawford said to come quick! It's Susan!'

CHAPTER ELEVEN

RICHARD raced to the kitchen dragging a stiff and struggling Megan behind him.

Jim was standing outside Susan's open door, his hands brushing against his eyes, his shoulders slumped forward in an attitude of hopelessness. But he pulled himself together and straightened at once when he saw them. 'Take Charlotte home with you, Franz,' he said quietly. 'I'll call you later.'

Franz nodded with immediate understanding and hustled Charlotte out of the door without a word.

When they had gone, Jim turned. 'I thought we'd never find you. She's dying, Richard. I don't know how she's lasted this long.' He glanced at his watch and shook his head. 'She's a fighter, I'll have to say that for her. She told me she can't let go until she sees you.'

A muscle clenched in Richard's jaw as he advanced on him. 'No!'

'You've got to see her.'

'Do you know what she did? I mean besides killing my father and Christina and almost killing Megan?'

Megan started to back away, but he reached behind him without taking his eyes off Jim and roughly curled his arm around her, hauling her possessively close to his side.

'She told her she was my wife, Jim. All this time Megan thought I was married—to Susan!'

Jim's astonished gaze flew to her face, then he looked helplessly back to Richard.

'So if you think I'm going in there and make things easier for her——'

Megan put her hand on his chest. 'Please, Richard. This may be your last chance. You've got to forgive her.'

'Forgive?' he exploded. '*Never!*'

She flinched at the absolute denial, and then she knew this fragile thing between them couldn't really be love. He was a man too cruel, too bent on revenge to be open to a lesser emotion such as love.

As the pulsing silence stretched and grew, she gave in to the bitter sense of disillusionment rising in her throat and stared straight into his eyes, knowing it had to be for the last time. This was the reality she had come out of the convent to face. Unbearable pain flickered across her face, but she kept her voice steady. 'Then this has to be goodbye, Richard.'

Much later that morning, after she had showered and changed into a white cotton sundress, Megan was standing at her bedroom window when an ambulance slowly pulled in the gravel drive, its lights and siren silent. She continued to stand there, shivering, long after it left. She wasn't going downstairs again. Jim would come for her when it was time to go. Her bag was packed; all she had to do was wait.

Everything was glowing and vibrant in the rainwashed countryside outside her window. The dark gnarled vines were bathed in sunshine. She thought of the innocent girl she had been when she first came here and the disillusioned woman she

was now. Was it worth it? she asked herself. There
was no answer.

Birds sang and crickets chirped in the green
grass. In the space of a rainstorm, everything had
changed. Her whole outlook had been turned
upside down and become clear. Her eyes were wide
open and she could see Richard for what he was: a
vengeful, unforgiving man of stone. It had been
sheer folly to imagine herself in love with him.
Love was supposed to be gentle and soft and warm
and comforting, not some crazy wild longing
coupled with a terrible breathlessness where she
didn't know right from wrong and was powerless
to choose between them. Her hands clenched
savagely on the windowsill. It never had been love;
he wasn't capable of it.

Everything inside her shrivelled to a frozen ball
of pain, when a sudden prickling at the back of her
neck made her turn. But it wasn't Jim as she
expected. Richard stood in the doorway, and her
whole body instinctively vibrated at his nearness.
His hair was damp from the shower he had taken,
his face was smoothly shaven. A clean white shirt
was partially unbuttoned and rolled back to his
elbows. His jeans were crisp, tapering down the
powerful length of his legs. All these things
registered on her consciousness, but she was
thrown by his sudden intent interest in the floor at
his booted feet. For a long time he kept his head
bent, his eyes down. Cold and remote and
chillingly blue, they shifted restlessly to some point
at the right of her, then the left. She finally realised
he was avoiding looking straight at her.

'Richard?' she whispered with a trembling sense
of dread.

He looked into her face then, the stillness

between them profound. He was quivering, his eyes full of pain, his steps almost faltering as he came closer.

'What is it?' she breathed.

'Why didn't you tell me? Did you enjoy laughing at me all this time?'

'Laughing? What are you talking about?'

'Susan knew. Jim knew. Why did you keep it from me?'

'What?' Her voice shook and she reached out to put a hand on his arm, but flinched when he jerked away from her touch.

'All this time you led me to believe you were so experienced with men. I thought you were a——' he sucked in his breath harshly, '—but all this time—you're a *nun*!'

Megan stood absolutely still, her jaw falling open soundlessly, her eyes locked with his. 'I led you to believe?' she breathed. '*I* led you?'

A dull red crept up his neck, burning his ears and staining his cheekbones before disappearing into his hair. 'All you had to do was tell me.'

'Is that right?' Her mouth thinned. 'And you would have believed me?'

He rubbed his hands over his eyes and dragged them across the back of his neck. 'That's why Susan had to see me before she died. She wanted to ask me to forgive her for telling the "nun who loved me" that she was my wife. Isn't that rich? She didn't want me to forgive her for the rest. She said my father's and Christina's deaths hadn't been deliberate, so she didn't need to be forgiven for them. But she set out to deceive you and she was sorry. I thought she was lying, that this was some new torture for me, but Jim told me it wasn't a lie. *He* knew!'

Megan couldn't look at the twisted anger in his face any more. Turning away, she pressed a hand to her mouth.

'Why didn't you tell me?' His voice was low and furious. 'You made me look like a fool!'

'I told you—but you never listened. There were never any other men. There was only you, no one else. Even this morning I told you, but you didn't believe me.'

'You didn't say you were a nun.'

'I'm not!' she flared, rounding on him.

'You told Susan you were. Even Jim agreed.'

'I told them I was raised in a convent. I wanted to become a nun. I even asked for permission to enter the order. But that was before——' She bit back the words.

Richard's head snapped back sharply, his whole body jerking to a stop. 'Before what?'

She tried to turn away, but he was looking at her strangely.

'Before you!' A smothered sob escaped her. 'You've ruined everything for me!'

His face whitened. 'There were just a few stolen kisses,' he said shakily. 'I never took your innocence. You can still be a nun.'

Her head moved from side to side. How could she explain that that part of her life was over? She couldn't go back to being the girl she was, even if she wanted to. How could she ever again be content with the simple contemplative life of a nun? Her heart would always be here in this valley—with Richard.

'No,' she sobbed. 'No, I'm not going back to the convent. There's no place for me there any more. I don't think there ever was.'

His arms came up to grip her shoulders. Even as

she steeled herself against the bruising pressure, he
checked the motion, his hands tautly hovering in
the air at her sides as if he didn't have the right to
touch her.

She was already swaying towards him, but had
to drag herself back and stand stiffly facing him.

'What, then?' His face was like chiselled stone.
'Where will you go? What will you do?'

'I don't know.' She dragged her eyes away from
him and looked at the paintings propped against
her suitcase on the floor. Her lips quivered. 'I
suppose I could sell those and start over
somewhere.'

Richard's hands fell lifelessly to his sides and he
grimly stepped away to see what she was talking
about.

There were two paintings. One was of Charlotte,
not as she was now but as she would be in a few
years' time, with her hair tumbling far down her
back and her vivid blue eyes alive and brilliant.
She wore a long pale blue dress starkly carved
against the curving softness of her body, billowing
out behind her as if she was standing in a strong
wind. One hand was shyly raised, beckoning. A
long finger of light slashed across the wasteland
behind her and she looked strangely abandoned,
but not forlorn. There was a certain stubborn
resilience in her stance, as if she would never allow
herself to be crushed by anything life handed to
her.

'My God,' Richard said softly, shaking his head.
'She'll look exactly like this soon—as long as I
don't try to deny her femininity.' His eyes swept to
Megan. 'A talent like this would be wasted in a
convent.'

'Not wasted. I was told I'd have to temper it.'

'That would be a crime. You've got a tremendous gift that shouldn't be tampered with.'

'Why?' Her breath was short and sharp when she looked him full in the face. 'What do you see that I don't? Mother Superior couldn't explain it, but she said my paintings showed I didn't belong in a convent. Why?'

He probed her face for a long minute before tearing his eyes away and pulling out the other painting.

It was of him, standing tall and straight, his carved features full of haughty dignity and pride. No background could do him justice, so she had set him in a muted landscape and had all the rugged power emanate from him. His unruly jet black hair shone and the skin on his face might not have been paint, it was so like living, breathing flesh. His eyes were vivid and alive with a hint of anguish in their depths. The deep furrows down the sides of his face were palpable. His full sensuous mouth only faintly smiled, but she had captured the bitterness that was always there. A rough blue cotton shirt was unbuttoned almost to his waist and the sleeves were rolled to the elbow, showing his tanned skin moistened with sweat. His big hands were clenched by his sides and his long legs were set wide apart, their strong muscles straining against the taut cloth of his dusty jeans.

He stared at the painting a few seconds longer and then Megan watched in fascination as his whole face began to alter when he set it down and turned to look at her. Deathly pale, with blue ridges at the sides of his mouth, the hard aloof mask began to fall away, leaving his expression naked and young and defenceless as she had never seen it.

'You flatter me,' he said softly, his eyes running over her face with a hungry brilliance.

Megan trembled and helplessly shook her head. 'It isn't flattery. I can only paint what I see.'

'Then you've been blinded by love. It's there in every brush stroke.' His breath bubbled harshly past his lips. 'I'm no good for you, Megan. I don't deserve to have you love me.'

She swallowed convulsively and tried to calm the sudden mad thumping of her heart as shock and amazement and disbelief followed one another. Taking a faltering step towards him, another and then another, she didn't stop until she was a breath away from him, her body almost touching his. 'Don't you think I should decide that for myself?'

'I thought you already had. It was there in your face when you told me goodbye. You thought I had no forgiveness in me.'

'I could have been wrong—about a lot of things.' Her heart began to sing wildly in a sudden irrational welling of joy. 'You saw Susan, didn't you?' she asked breathlessly, already knowing the answer.

Richard nodded slowly, looking at her.

'And seeing her, you had to forgive her.' It was a statement, not a question. 'I know you did. I just know it.'

A slight tremor went through him. 'I asked her to forgive me too, Megan.'

She stared at him, racked by hot and cold shudders. What a blow to his pride! She knew what it must have cost him to do that. And then she knew, beyond a shadow of a doubt, that he had done it for her, to prove to himself and her that he was capable of forgiving—thus, loving.

Painfully aware of her own inexperience, she hesitated only a moment before leaning her rigid body towards him, and then, unable to restrain the impulse, put both her hands at the sides of his face and pulled it down to hers, uncertainly pressing a timid kiss to his bluish lips.

His hands were hanging lifelessly at his sides and for an instant he left them there until she daringly touched the tip of her tongue to the strong rigid line of his mouth. That was his undoing. With a strangled groan, his arms came right around her, crushing her whole body to his burning length, shaken by the quick surge of passion flaring between them, welding them together.

Guided by pure instinct, Megan's hands slid into his hair, loving the way the black silk clung to her fingers. Pure sensation made her bones melt when she felt him tremble against her. Mindlessly shivering with pleasure, she felt an involuntary moan of wild sweet longing rise in her throat as his kiss became deep and searching and rough with possession.

When his plundering mouth left hers to explore the long soft curve of her neck, his caressing hands sped up and down her spine, making her shiver.

She was trembling so violently she nearly fell but he managed to pull himself away from her and she stood, swaying, staring into his eyes for endless reeling seconds.

'I'm sorry, Megan.' His voice shook. 'I must frighten you when I kiss you like that—but, God!' he sucked in a deep breath, 'I can't help myself.'

Her eyes widened. 'Frighten? You don't frighten me. I frighten myself.'

He smiled helplessly and it made him look so

young and boyish. 'You told me that once before, but I thought it was an act. Forgive me—I should have known. I think I did know, but I didn't want to accept that you were for real. It was much easier to think of you as a—woman of—easy virtue.'

A brilliant wash of red ran up her neck. 'Don't start picking and choosing your words now. I liked you better before—when you thought I was a hiker.'

Richard's jaw started to drop.

'I have heard about such things, you know,' she said airily, 'and I even met one, the same day I met you.'

A delighted laugh rumbled deep in his chest, bubbling up and breaking free and his eyes glowed like brilliant blue diamonds. He reached for her hands and linked his fingers with hers, laughing softly. 'The word is "hooker", not "hiker".'

'Oh,' said Megan sheepishly, bending her head to let her flaming hair cover the fire in her face. 'I've led a very sheltered life. I was hoping you'd teach me all the things I've missed.'

He gently drew her to him and rested his forehead against hers, holding her in the strong tight circle of his arms. 'Things like that you don't need to know, but I'll tell you about them if you're curious. I'd rather concentrate on marrying you and having you teach Charlotte and me all about love. I haven't done a very good job of raising my daughter so far.'

'But I don't know anything about love,' she protested. 'I'm just learning myself.'

'It's there in your paintings,' Richard said gravely. 'That's what your Mother Superior must have seen.' His face changed, became unbearably gentle. 'Jim told me about you being abandoned when you were little and how you've never known love the way we know it. But it's there, Megan. Maybe we can find it together?'

'Oh, I'd like that,' she said, her eyes shining with trust. 'And I do want to marry you—so much.' Her hands slipped inside his unbuttoned shirt and curled into his muscular chest, making him quiver.

'You know,' he said unsteadily, 'for somebody who's never known a man, you catch on awfully quick!'

'I'm just trying some of the things you've already taught me.' Her lips started to follow her hands and he was forced to pull away from her.

'Stop, Megan, while I can still keep my intentions honourable!'

Her pulse was pounding and she had difficulty breathing. 'I liked you better when they weren't.'

'You shouldn't say things like that,' he murmured thickly, taking her hands and crushing them in his. After a minute he had himself in control again. 'Is there someone whose permission I have to get before I can marry you?'

'No,' she said softly. 'I'm completely yours.'

Richard groaned, dropping her hands as if she had burned him.

'I'm sorry,' she choked. 'I didn't mean——'

'Oh God, Megan! I'm not made of stone. You accused me of not treating you with respect, but when you say things like that, it's so damned——' he caught himself, '—darned—hard to keep my hands off . . .'

Megan pressed her fingers to his lips to make him stop. 'I love you, Richard. I'm sorry.' She stepped away from him and demurely bent her head, calling a halt to her unknowing provocation.

'Come on,' he murmured thickly, twining the fingers of one hand with hers and picking up her suitcase with the other. 'We'll get Jim to make arrangements for blood tests and get a licence—now—or else I'll be begging for your forgiveness too.'

'I'll always forgive you,' she smiled, following him down the stairs. 'If you'll forgive me.'

'Always, Megan. Always.'

It was more than a promise.

THE Leo Man
Rebecca Stratton

Harlequin Romance

THE Winds of Winter
Sandra Field

Harlequin Romance

Love Beyond Reason
Karen van der Zee

Harlequin Romance

Man of Power
Mary Wibberley

Harlequin Romance

4 FREE
Harlequin Romances

Enter a uniquely exciting new world with

Harlequin American Romance ™

Harlequin American Romances are the first romances to explore today's love relationships. These compelling novels reach into the hearts and minds of women across America... probing the most intimate moments of romance, love and desire.

You'll follow romantic heroines and irresistible men as they boldly face confusing choices. Career first, love later? Love without marriage? Long-distance relationships? All the experiences that make love real are captured in the tender, loving pages of **Harlequin American Romances.**

What makes American women so different when it comes to love? Find out with **Harlequin American Romance!**

Send for your introductory FREE book now!

Get this book FREE!

Mail to:

Harlequin Reader Service

In the U.S.	In Canada
2504 West Southern Ave.	P.O. Box 2800, Postal Station A
Tempe, AZ 85282	5170 Yonge St., Willowdale, Ont. M2N 6J3

YES! I want to be one of the first to discover **Harlequin American Romance.** Send me FREE and without obligation *Twice in a Lifetime.* If you do not hear from me after I have examined my FREE book, please send me the 4 new **Harlequin American Romances** each month as soon as they come off the presses. I understand that I will be billed only $2.25 for each book (total $9.00). There are no shipping or handling charges. There is no minimum number of books that I have to purchase. In fact, I may cancel this arrangement at any time. *Twice in a Lifetime* is mine to keep as a FREE gift, even if I do not buy any additional books. **154 BPA NAZE**

Name	(please print)	

Address		Apt. no.

City	State/Prov.	Zip/Postal Code

Signature (If under 18, parent or guardian must sign.)

This offer is limited to one order per household and not valid to current Harlequin American Romance subscribers. We reserve the right to exercise discretion in granting membership. If price changes are necessary, you will be notified.
Offer expires September 30, 1985

AMR-SUB-2